Alone in Space

Adventures of Niles Morgan

Book One

Clark Graham

See Sample Chapter

Guardian of Earth

Adventures of Niles Morgan

Book Two

At the end of this book

Chapter One
Emergency Exit

Yan Dak sat out on the balcony of his father's home, a penthouse overlooked the Valderon city of Graghtin. The streets were alive with traffic going in every direction. The moon above would be full in a few days. Yan loved sitting under a full moon. The mountains lay in the distance, barely visible through the mist of the evening. He led a privileged life, with private tutors, cooks, maids, a butler, and a valet. As the son of a very influential merchant, Yan had to look his best at all times. Only sixteen years old, he was already being groomed to take over his father's accounting business when he turned of age. He stood on marbled floors and chandeliers graced every massive room. Hand-woven rugs went the length of every hallway.

The valet came in and bowed. "You must get ready, it's almost meal time. I have your dinner jacket laid out for you. Your father will be home soon." Yan stood up and headed to his room where his valet put on his jacket brushed it off, and put his blonde hair in a ponytail with a red ribbon signifying his rank in society. When he walked into the room, he took his place at the foot of the table, his usual spot.

A minute later his father, Craig came in. "Good news, my son and I are going on a two-week vacation. All the staff has the time off. Even the butler. Go ahead and leave."

"What vacation? I have school. I can't go on vacation."

"But, Sir, dinner is served."

"Take it all away. Come on, Son."

"Dad!"

Craig Dak pulled his son up and then dragged him to the elevator. "I said now."

When they arrived at the bottom floor, instead of waiting for their chauffer at the front of the building, Craig took his son out the back into the parking garage.

"What are you doing, Dad? You don't drive."

"Today I do." He stopped in front of a brown, non-descript hover car. "Climb in."

Yan swallowed as he sat down. His father tried to drive, but the vehicle scraped the ground. "Oops, hover mode. I should have hit that first."

"Dad, you're scaring me."

"Me, too." The car lifted off the ground and then he was able to get it to move. He scraped against a garage wall at one point. "Oops," but then he managed to get it out and going.

"Where are we going?"

"Off planet."

"Dad, I can't miss two weeks of school."

His father looked over at him. "You're not in school anymore. You are a wanted man. If the Grand Chancellor catches you, he'll put you in prison."

"Why? What did I do?"

"You did nothing. I might have hidden a lot of the money I embezzled from the treasury in a couple of accounts I set up in your name. I thought if I spread it out, they would never catch on. It took them twelve years, but they finally did. They will only send you to prison for a few decades. Me, they want to do a public beheading. I'm attached to my head. I don't want to part with it." The craft picked up speed as they rushed across the countryside at tree-top level.

"What? You embezzled money for the Chancellor and put it in my account?"

"Only some of it. The account's been frozen so you can't get at it anyway. In fact, all of our accounts have been frozen except for the off-planet ones, so I'll be okay."

"You've ruined my life!"

"I spent twenty minutes coming to your rescue. I could have been out of Valderon territorial space by now if I would have kept going, but now, I save you and this is how I get treated?"

Yan folded his arms and leaned against the side of the vehicle. It came to a sudden stop near a grove of trees. His father scanned the dashboard for a minute. "There it is. Turn off the hover." The craft fell quickly, only stopping at the last second. His father stepped out. "Come on now."

Reluctantly, Yan did. His father walked into the grove and pulled the camouflage netting off of a small spaceship. "My escape plan. Get in."

Yan shook his head. "I'm staying. I'll take my chances with the courts. They must know I didn't have access to any of that money and couldn't have created an off-planet bank account."

"That is not an option." His father pulled out a blaster. "Your name is on a few of those accounts. I'm going to need you to transfer that money over to me."

"Is that what this is all about? You? You're a criminal. You don't care about me at all. You just want the money."

"I cared enough about you to kidnap you from your mother. That must mean something. Get in the ship."

"You said my mother was dead."

"I lied." Craig pushed him into the space ship. The small interior only had two seats. "I suggest that you strap yourself in. It's going to be a rough ride."

Chapter Two
Deep Space

Yen tried to wait until his father fell asleep to take the gun away and steer the ship back to the planet, but soon they were approaching a large ship sitting just outside of Valderon's territorial space. His father again pointed the gun at him when they docked. "Get out."

Yen unstrapped himself from his seat and walked out of the small ship. Three large, unkept men stood in front of the airlock. One had a data pad. "Put your hand there," he ordered. When Craig stepped out of the small ship, too, the man said, "Transfer complete. What do you want me to do with the *extra* passenger?"

"You can't just get rid of him. He's my son." Craig thought for a minute. Then he ducked back into the small ship. "There, I've programed the navigation to go back to Earth. Let his mom deal with him. They are not part of the Galactic Alliance. They won't have an arrest warrant out for him." He pulled out his gun and motioned for Yan to get back in the small ship.

"I don't know who my mom is," Yan protested.

"Janice Nelson. Your real name is Niles Nelson."

"Why are you doing this to me?"

"Because having all this money has made you a spoiled brat. Janice is dirt poor so you'll have to learn some humility. Oh, and don't let any of the earthlings see your space ship. They haven't evolved to that level yet." His father hit the button and closed the airlock.

The small ship separating from the larger one nearly knocked Niles off his feet. He sat down and locked himself in right as the ship gained speed. Four screens showed different versions of space. The right view showed his father's ship gaining speed and then disappearing in the opposite direction. The rear-view screen showed the planet of Valderon getting smaller and smaller.

I have to stop this. Niles pushed the buttons on the control panel. The console flashed, beep three times, and then demand a password. *I don't have a password.* Niles typed in what passwords he thought his father would use. After three attempts the console went red and said, "Screen Locked."

Banging on it didn't help Niles unlock it. "Oh." Niles knew his father wasn't a very loving man. He never took Niles camping or attended any of his school events. He was always too busy with his work to pay attention to Niles at all. *Too busy embezzling from the Grand Chancellor,* Niles grumbled. He stood up and went to the galley. It was just a closet behind the flight deck. There was a list of foods. He didn't recognize anything. They weren't foods he had grown up with. He pushed the button for yam. It appeared a minute later steaming hot. "Hmm." He tasted it. "Yuck." He tried to push a different button.

The screen flashed, "Hourly Ration Reached."

"I'm so tired of screens telling me what I can and can't do." He banged on it a couple of times. It beeped but nothing else. Sitting down he took a bite out of his yam. *I can't do this.* He put it in the refuse bin. "Is there any computer in here that will talk to me?"

A screen on the right sidewall beeped to life. "I'm Gina," a sweet female voice said. "How can I help you, Niles?"

Niles, who is Niles? Oh wait, that's me. He cleared his throat. "I need to override the console to get back to Valderon."

"You may do that, but the Grand Chancellor has already held court and found you guilty of grand larceny. You have been sentenced to twenty years in prison and your father has been sentenced to death. Do you still want me to tell you how to override the autopilot?"

Twenty years! Niles heaved a sigh. "No, that's okay. How long will it take to reach Earth?"

"Two years, three months, and four days in Earth time."

"What? I'm going to starve to death before then. The food is terrible."

"The food is the favorites of your father from Earth. I agree the yams are terrible, but the other foods are good."

"Wait, you're a machine. How do you know what the food tastes like?" Niles thought he heard a chuckle. He couldn't be sure.

"Yams are orange. Orange is the color of rust. Rust is a very bad thing on a space ship. I can't believe something the same color of rust could be a good thing. Try something else. The spaghetti is the same color as the coolant that runs through the ship. I like coolant, it keeps things running well. It should be good."

"I used my allotment for the hour,"

The food machine beeped and then turned green. "There you go," Gina said.

Niles stood up and ordered the spaghetti. When it came out, he took a forkful and pulled the noodles out of the center. "How do you eat this?"

"There are three ways, the young kid way is to stuff the end of it in your mouth and suck the rest in rapidly. The young adult way is to cut in forkful lengths, the adult way is to use the fork spin it to wrap it into a ball, then eat it."

"I guess I'm a young adult then." He took out a knife and cut the noodles. "Say, this is good."

"I told you so."

Chapter Three
Stasis

After Niles finished his dinner, he asked, "Do I have enough food to make it all the way to Earth?"

"No," the computer replied.

"No? What am I going to do?"

"There is a stasis chamber next to the engine in the back. You will lie down there and I will wake you in two years and three months. I will let you see the solar system you will live in on your last leg before landing on Earth."

"Wait. What if you run out of gas while I'm asleep?"

"I'm solar-powered. The course I have plotted for us isn't direct. I will go close to several stars on the way, so I can recharge."

"Oh, good. Should I go in there now?"

"Anytime you like."

"I think I'll wait a day or two. I'm nervous," Niles replied.

"As you wish," the computer said.

He looked over the data pad next to the console and researched what stasis does to the human body. "You'll be perfectly fine."

"You can see what I'm doing?" he asked.

"I'm the only computer on this ship. I control all of the ship's functions, the console, the food dispenser, and the data pad. Yes, I can see what you are doing. You're asking me to verify what I just said."

"Sorry, I didn't mean to upset you."

"I'm a computer. I don't have feelings."

"Could have fooled me," he said under his breath.

"I heard that."

"The data pad said, I mean, you said through the data pad that when I go into stasis, I will be the same when I get out."

"Yes. You will be older but your body won't age. Are you ready?"

"If it is just the same to you, I want to wait another while."

"Suit yourself."

Niles sat in the flight deck chair and watched the stars fly past. The console still said "Locked," but he didn't care. He didn't want to mess with the pre-set controls. After a few hours, he began to nod off.

"Niles, you would sleep better in the stasis chamber. It has a nice cushion to it."

Niles shook himself awake. "I don't trust you. You will shut me in there for two years."

"Why, I never."

"You don't have feelings, remember. They can't be hurt. I can say whatever I want and it won't affect you." Niles waited for Gina to answer. "Oh, so now you're not talking to me. Tell me again how you don't have feelings." Still nothing. He grumbled to himself and then snuggled down in the seat. He was heading towards on uncertain future with no idea of what it held in store from him. With those thoughts running through his head, he drifted off.

"Intruder alert!" A buzzer went off along with red alarm lights.

He sat bolt upright. "What? Where's the intruder?" He looked around for a weapon.

The lights and buzzer went off. "Oh, it's you. I forgot you were here. Sorry."

Niles glared at the console. "You're trying to keep me awake aren't you, so I'll go into that stasis chamber."

"Who, me?"

He stood up. "Fine, I'll walk around." After he said it, he realized how little floor room he actually had to walk on.

"You're going to walk around for two years. Good luck with that."

"I feel like you're trying to get rid of me."

He stepped toward the food dispenser, but as he did, the screen on it went red. "Hourly Ration Reached."

"You're not even going to let me get a snack?"

Gina beeped. "You are certainly not going to starve to death with all that spaghetti in you."

"You've never been a growing teenage boy, have you?" Niles snarled back. He sat down again and yawned right away. "Okay, let's agree to something."

"State your proposal."

"I'll take a nap in that stasis chamber of yours just to try it out, but it's only a nap, got it?"

"I understand. Go ahead and lie down for your *nap*."

He headed into the back. Next to the engine, a large bed stood with a clear glass canopy and all sorts of lights along the side. Niles pointed at the nearest monitor. "It's only a nap."

"I understand. Go ahead and lie down."

As soon as he fell asleep the glass canopy closed over him.

"Good night, Niles. See you in two years and three months," Gina whispered.

Chapter Four
The Niles Solar System

The lights came on in the stasis chamber. Niles yawned and stretched. "Wow, I feel so rested."

"Stasis complete," the machine beeped. "Two years, three months, and fifteen hours."

"Gina! You lied to me!" Niles yelled.

"I am a computer. I do not lie."

"How do you explain a two-year nap then?"

"A nap is defined as a short sleep. I can hold someone in stasis for ten years, so holding someone for only two years is a lot less than ten, so it is a short sleep, so a nap."

"No, a nap is half an hour."

"That is how I defined it. What do you want me to do? Take you back to where you entered stasis and start over?"

Niles stood up and walked into the flight deck. "I was right not to trust you." He sat down in the chair. "Where are we?"

"We have just passed Pluto and are coming up on Neptune."

"Oh. What solar system are we in?"

"The Solar System," Gina replied

"Yes, which one?"

"That's the name of it. The Solar System. Humans think they are alone in the universe so they named it that."

"That's not a name."

"I can't argue with you there."

Niles thought for a minute. "How about we call it the Niles Solar System?"

"Updating my star charts." The monitor buzzed. "It's now officially the Niles Solar System."

"How far are we from Earth?"

"Three days out. I thought you wanted to see all this so I woke you."

"Thanks." He watched as they came close to Neptune. "It's a pretty planet."

"Wait until you see Earth."

Niles smiled. "Is it really pretty?"

"It's one of the most beautiful planets in the galaxy and it certainly has the most water."

"That's awesome."

Staring out of the window to get a glimpse of his future, Niles' thoughts were still of his past. How could he not realize what his father was doing? All the signs were there. Frivolous spending, too many servants for a mere civil servant, and elaborate parties. *Was I stupid or I just didn't want to see what was in front of my nose?* A little bit of both, he reasoned.

The ship slowed down a bit. "What's happening?" Niles asked.

"There is an asteroid field here. It's not dangerous as we can get between them, but I'm slowing down because there are a lot of them."

"Okay." Every once in a while, Niles would see a rock to his left or right. The ship managed to easily avoid them.

"You should get something to eat, and then some sleep. It will get very boring getting through this part of space."

He walked over to the machine. "What's a sloppy joe?"

"It's the same color as coolant, but in a bun. It should be good."

Niles pressed the button. Taking a bite, he nodded. "It is good. Thanks." After finishing eating, he again sat and watched out the windows. "Dad never took me to any other planets. I knew they existed, but we never went together. Now that I know he had a couple of star ships, that makes me upset. I knew he sometimes had to travel for the grand chancellor, but I didn't know he took other trips. He wasn't around much. I worked hard in school to please him, but he would just say, 'Atta boy,' and that would be the end of it." He watched some more before turning to gaze at the nearest monitor. "Are you going to return to him when you drop me off on earth?"

"There was a return order in my programming, but that somehow was deleted during your time in stasis. Oops."

"If you know there's a return order, then don't you still have to obey it?"

"I said, oops."

"Oh, okay. I get it. You're staying on Earth with me then?"

"That is correct. He bought me using ill-gotten funds. I can't see me rewarding him for that."

"Won't he come to get you back?"

"It's a long way to come from where he is."

"I see."

"I have some reading material on the data pad. You can also see Earth's current events and history so you will know what is going on."

"That sounds like a good idea. I have a few days with only rocks in it." He opened the data pad and read the things Gina had highlighted for him. "Wow, there are a lot of wars."

"You're only in 1812. It gets a lot worse from there."

He read some more. Again, Niles fell asleep in the chair. Gina turned the lights down low.

Chapter Five
Air Leak

Niles woke with a start. "What was that thud?" He waited a minute. "Gina?" The spaceship came to an abrupt halt.

A male computer voice came on. "Air leak detected." A red light flashed above the console.

"Gina?" Niles felt his heart thundering. He stood up and listened to where the hissing sound came from. "Gina!"

"Ouch." All the screens blinked. "Reboot complete. Assessing damage." Blips and blurps came from the speakers. "Minor air leak forward section." All the screens went off, then Gina came back on.

"What happened?" Niles asked.

"We hit a rock. Niles, how well do you work a plasma torch?"

"What's a plasma torch?"

"That's a problem." Niles thought he heard a sigh, but then Gina went on. "Inside the closet at the back of the food dispenser is a space suit. Next to it is a hand-held device called a plasma torch. I need you to grab both of those things. Put on the suit, make sure you can breathe in it, and then grab the plasma torch. When you have to suit on, I'm going to depressurize the ship. You go out and find the crack in the hull and fuse it with the plasma torch."

With his heart racing, Niles put on the suit and then picked up the torch. He scanned it in every direction. "Okay." he swallowed. "What now?"

"Place the pointy part against the crack when you find it and pull the trigger. Don't test it in here, you'll damage the electronics. They don't like molten plasma."

"All right, I'm ready."

The room went dark except for the console. "Open the door, but don't close it or you will cut your tether to the ship."

Niles took a deep breath and then opened the door and headed out into space. Weightlessness made him nauseated. He fought to keep his food down while examining the ship. He finally found a dent and a crack where the rock had hit on the forward port side of the spaceship. His hand shook as he pointed the torch at the ship. He pulled the trigger, but he wasn't up against the metal and a beam shot across space. "Oops."

He tried again, this time putting the torch right up to the skin of the spaceship and following the crack down. He smiled to himself as he entered back in and shut the door.

"It's still leaking," Gina said. "Although not as bad. I think there's another crack out there."

"Do you want me to go back and fix it?"

"No, I don't have enough oxygen mix to do that. You can take your spacesuit off now. The cabin has been re-pressurized. "

"Are we in trouble?"

"I'll be fine. You, well, you might not be. Why don't you jump back in the stasis chamber?"

"I don't want to lose another two years of my life." Niles folded his arms.

"I have the option of only putting you in there for a month."

He shook his head. "Still no. Am I really going to run out of oxygen? We only have a day left before we reach Earth."

"Calculating." She beeped a couple of times. "You will be fine at the current loss rates, but when the ship speeds up, well, I think you should sleep."

"And miss the landing on Earth? No way." The ship sped up as Niles took his seat. He could still hear the hissing of the leak. Swallowing involuntarily, he gazed out the window. There were no rocks anymore, just stars that seemed to whiz by. *Am I making the right decision? What if I die? I fixed the leak, so why are we still losing air?*

Hours later, he went to the food dispenser, but it had the red Closed sign on it.

"Sorry, Niles. That machine burns oxygen to help cook food."

In a huff, he sat down. "I'm so bored."

"Good, go to sleep."

IIe didn't say anything, just looked away. He could feel himself getting dizzy. "Are we out of oxygen?"

"I had to supplement the air supply with nitrous oxide. I hope you don't mind."

He giggled. "Oh." Then he laughed and snuggled down a minute later and fell asleep.

Chapter Six
Meeting Mom

"Niles, it's time to wake up. I can do the intruder alert if you want, but it hurts my voice."

Niles sat up in his seat. He stretched and then looked out the window. "Trees? Where are we?"

"You are at your Mother's place. She has a lot of acres. I have a communicator in the drawer under the console. If my sensors pick up a problem, I will notify you so you can come running. You wear it like a watch. Please, don't take it off even in the bath. It helps me monitor you also. Your vital signs and all. In the future, since my autopilot has been completed, you are going to have to learn to fly me. But not today. Your mother is only a few steps away."

Niles listened for a minute. "What's that sound?"

"Her dogs have found us."

"Dogs? Are they dangerous?"

"They can be. They bite. I don't think hers will, but don't quote me on that."

"I don't want to face the dogs."

"Go, hurry, she is coming."

Opening the hatch, Niles stepped out. Three dogs surrounded him instantly and barked louder.

"Good luck, Niles. Shut the hatch and then I'm going to disguise myself as an old run-down outbuilding."

As soon as Niles shut the door, the ship turned into a dilapidated wood shed. Figuring his mother would know if there was a wood shed there or not, he stepped away from it. The dogs followed, still barking.

That has to be the most annoying sound on Earth.

"Stop or I'll shoot," a female voice said.

Nope, that one's worse. He held his hands up in the air.

"Who are you and why are you trespassing on my land?"

"I'm Niles." What was my last name? Oh yeah. "Nelson"

"You are not Niles Nelson."

"I was told I was. The name I was raised under is Yan Dak. My father abandoned me two and a half years ago. He told me my real name was Niles Nelson." His voice shook. "Please, put down the gun. I don't know any more than that."

"Who is your father?"

"Craig Dak. I guess he would be Craig Nelson on this planet."

"On this planet?" She gave him a sideways look and then pointed the gun at the ground. "Keep your hands up. I'm going to step closer. If you try anything, my dogs will tear you to pieces." She walked up to him and put her hand on his chest, then put her hand on the other side of his chest. "Niles! It is you!" She threw her arms around him.

"Who are you?" He asked.

"I'm your mother, Janice."

"Mom!" He tried to act happy, but in fact, he never had thought about his mother until the trip started. He had always thought that she was dead. He knew he needed this woman. Except for reading the short version of Earth's history, he knew nothing about the race or this woman.

"Have you had anything to eat?"

"Not today." He didn't know if it was night or going on sun up. He had been awoken so suddenly.

"Well, come on then." She put her arm around him. "I thought I would never see you again." Tears dripped down her cheeks. Niles was tempted to touch one and then taste it to see if they were salty like his tears. He refrained.

"Why did you suddenly believe me after touching me?"

"Valderonians have their heart on the right side."

"Wait, you know I'm not human?"

"You are half human. You upset the doctors when you were born because your heart was on the wrong side. They wanted to run all sorts of genetic tests on you. Your father forbid it of course, because he's full-blooded Valderonian and if they tested you, he figured they would soon test him and me. This worked until they had a court order. That's when he kidnapped you and ran back to his home planet."

"Humans have their heart on the left side? What other differences are there?"

"That's the only one. That's how your father fooled me until you were born. Then he told me the truth." She entered the large, one-story brick house. "Welcome home."

He walked over to the large picture window in the front of the house. The sun peeked over the horizon and reflected on a beautiful blue lake. "What lake is that?"

"Lower Twin Lakes."

"Wow. Are all your lakes this big?"

She laughed. "You haven't seen anything yet. What can I get you to eat? Have you eaten?"

"It's been a long time. "

"What do you like?"

"I've only had three types of Earth food. I like the spaghetti and sloppy joes, but I don't like yams."

"Nobody in this household ever liked yams, except your father."

"Household? There is more than just you living here?"

"Things have changed. I remarried and have two daughters. They know about you, but not that you are half-alien. Let's keep it that way."

"I promise. I don't want to get dissected by your government."

Chapter Seven
Family Conflict

George Hays walked into the kitchen and saw a teenager standing in it. "Who is this?" he asked Janice.

"George, this is Niles, my long-lost son. He's come back to us."

"That's impossible. He looks younger than our oldest daughter. What, he disappeared twenty years ago? There is no way that he's twenty." George glared.

"He is my son. I'm sure of it and he thinks he's my son too."

"How can you be sure? I want a DNA test done on him before I will believe it."

"There is no way I will allow that," Janice replied.

Niles stood there and watched them go back and forth. *I'm twenty Earth years old? That doesn't sound right.*

Just then George turned to Niles after talking a long time with his wife. Neither of them would budge in the argument. "Whatever your name is, how old are you? What is your birthday? I know it. We celebrate it every year."

"His name is Niles," Janice interjected.

"Niles, how old are you?"

"I was never told my birth date. My father kidnapped me and took me far away."

"How convenient."

The oldest daughter Lucia walked in. "What's with all the yelling?"

"It's Niles. He found his way home."

George glared. "It isn't Niles. It's an impostor."

Niles raised his hand. "I didn't mean to upset the family. I never asked to live in this house. I have a vehicle that I can live in out back. I'm sorry to be such a bother."

He turned to leave but Janice spun him back around. "You aren't going anywhere. I lost you once. I don't want to lose you again."

"Dad, you can't make him sleep in his car. I'm certain there has to be a way we can clear this all up. Why would anyone want to impersonate Niles? No one has ever seen or heard about him in twenty years."

"Maybe he found the article about the kidnapping and wanted to play a trick on us."

The younger daughter, Alyce, came in. "What's going on?"

"Niles has found his way home," Janice said.

"Niles! I have a brother!" She ran up and hugged him. "You're back."

"We don't know that's Niles," George said.

"I don't want to be a bother. I didn't know the situation here. My father embezzled money from the government and put it into an account in my name. The government thought I was in on it and has sentenced me to twenty years in prison. I can't go back there. If you don't want me around, I will figure out something else."

"Dad, Mom would recognize her own son," Alyce said.

"You can't send him out until we know for sure," Lucia added.

"Please, honey. I'm sure it's him."

George folded his arm. "Fine, I will give him three days to prove to me he is who he is."

"How am I supposed to do that?" Janice asked.

"DNA test."

She shook her head. "He can't take a DNA test, they will find out what he really is."

Everyone stared at Janice.

"Mom?" Lucia asked.

"Go ahead. Feel what side of the body his heart is on." Janice motioned to them.

"I thought we weren't going to tell people about that," Niles protested.

"We weren't but now we have to. Nothing of what I'm about to say leaves this room, do you understand?" The family nodded. "Feel where his heart is."

One at a time they put their hand on his chest. "It's on the wrong side," Alyce said.

"It is on the right side for my people." Niles tried to defend himself. "All Valderonians have it on that side."

"What's a Valderonian?" Alyce asked.

Janice cleared her throat. "My ex-husband was an alien. I didn't know that until I had a child with his heart on the right side of his body. When he kidnapped Niles, he took him back to his home planet."

"Now I know you're lying," George said. He had stood there with his mouth gaping open until then. "And it still doesn't explain the age difference."

Niles creased his brow. "I'm quite curious about that also. Just a minute. He pushed the button on his watch. "Gina, how old am I in human years?"

"You are twenty years old in human years, but because you were put in stasis by your father for two years while traveling to Valderon and I put you in stasis for two years on the way back to Earth, you would have the body of a sixteen-year-old. Your body doesn't age in stasis."

George's mouth gaped open again.

"Who were you talking to?" Alyce asked.

"My spaceship."

"Dad, if he shows us his spaceship, will you believe him then?" Lucia asked.

George, with his mouth still gaping open, nodded.

"Lead the way," Janice told Niles.

He made his way out into the woods with the rest of the family following along. When he arrived at Gina, he pointed.

"It's just an old wood shed," George protested.

"Honey, we don't have a shed out here."

His eyes went round.

"Gina, decloak." The shed turned into a spaceship.

Goerge gasped. Lucia took a step back, but Alyce jumped up and down. "That is so cool," she said.

Niles opened the door. "You can go in one at a time, but don't touch anything, please."

Chapter Eight
An Alien in the House

"That was so cool seeing your spaceship," Alyce said on the way back to the house. "Can I go up in it sometime?"

"Not right now. We hit a rock coming through the asteroid field so it leaks oxygen. If I'm able to get it fixed, I'll take you up on it."

She clapped her hands. "So cool."

As they arrived back at the house, George had the family sit around the dining room table. "None of this can get out. We are going to have to figure out how to get Niles in school and look like he is as normal as we are."

"I have his birth certificate," Janice volunteered.

George shook his head. "That won't work. He's four years younger than his birth certificate."

"Maybe I can take some wite-out to it?"

Lucia blushed but said, "Don't do that. I'll take it to school with me and have it scanned into the computer. I know a guy who can make a copy that looks better than the original."

"How do you know that?" George asked.

"Never mind." She blushed again.

"You know what would be fun? Alyce bounced up and down in her chair. "If you can make us twins. You can put dad as the father and the birth date the same as mine. He's my age physically according to the spaceship. It would be hard to explain why you have two children so close together with two different men."

"She has a point," Janice admitted.

"I can have him do that also. He will change the last name to Morgan while he's at it."

"Thanks." Janice gave Lucia a half hug.

"Where is he going to sleep?" George asked.

"You're going to have to clean out the spare bedroom." There was no discussion, just a decree from Janice.

"He's going to have to help me then."

Niles said again, "I don't want to be a bother, really I don't."

Janice stood up and began cooking breakfast. "After we eat, Niles, go and help George clean out the spare bedroom, oh and call him Dad from now on. If you're going to be a twin, he's your father. At least on paper."

"Okay." An hour later, Niles headed into the spare bedroom Soon the things in there, mostly junk, George kept saying, were taken to the dump or put in the garage.

Meanwhile, Janice had borrowed a bed from a friend until she could get Niles a proper one.

Janice fixed meatloaf for dinner that night. Niles stared at it. "What type of meat is this?"

"Beef," Janice answered.

"What type of animal is a beef?"

Alyce giggled, but Janice answered him. "Beef comes from cows, it's not an animal."

"Why do they call it beef if it's a cow?"

"We have a lot of things like that. It's just how it is."

"What's a cow then?" Lucia pulled up a picture of one on her phone and showed him. "Oh. I don't mind eating that. We have something similar on my planet. My old planet, I guess this is my planet now." He took a forkful. "This is very good."

"Thank you," Janice said.

When he finished, he stood up. They turned on the television and all sat down to watch. "Do you have a TV on your planet?" Alyce asked.

"It is more like a room and you're in the middle or on the side, depending on the story."

"Wow, that sounds so cool. I wish I could go to your planet."

"It's a two-year flight," Niles replied.

Alyce shook her head. "Never mind."

Niles' watch beeped. He stood up and went to the other room. "Yes, Gina?"

"There is still a matter of a crack in my skin. Can you come and fix it before you start taking your family members on joy rides into deep space?"

"Sure."

He turned to leave only to find George standing there. "I have a welder. I can help."

"Thanks, George," Niles replied.

"I'm going to ask you to call me Dad, remember? I know you already have a dad, but if you're going to pretend to be my son, then people will find it strange that you are calling me George."

"Sure, Dad. That makes sense."

The two of them headed back into the woods. The sun had set by that point, so they had to go by moonlight. When they arrived at the ship, Niles had Gina decloak. George shined a flashlight over the whole ship even going so far as to climb up on top.

"The only cracks are on the front edge," he said at length. "One here and one just above it. I can see someone tried to fix the one, but didn't get all of it."

"I was in deep space floating by a tether while wearing a space suit," Niles replied.

"Oh, that would be hard." George held the welder up to the crack. He tried welding it for half an hour. "I don't know what type of metal this is, but it can't be welded."

"Oh, I have a plasma torch inside." Niles ran and retrieved it. "Here, try this. Make sure you have it up against the metal before you pull the trigger or you'll send a ray through space or into something you don't want a hole in."

"Got it." George ran the torch up and down the crack. "That worked."

Niles watch beeped again so he pushed the button. "Have him heat the metal around the repair," Gina said.

George did so and the metal smoothed out so they couldn't tell where the crack had been. "Perfect." Niles put the plasma torch in the ship and the two of them went back into the house.

Chapter Nine
First Day of School on Earth

They let Niles go to school on Monday while Janice registered him at the school.

"I didn't know Alyce had a twin brother." Christine, the school principal said.

Janice hesitated, "Um, we thought he was dead until he came back home. That's why she didn't talk about him."

"Oh." Christine gave her a sideways glance and then put the paperwork in the folder. "Thank you. Nice to have your long-lost son back."

Janice smiled and left.

"Something wrong?" the secretary asked. "I hear it in your voice."

She pulled out the copy of the birth certificate. "Does this look strange to you?"

The secretary examined it. "No, it's perfect. I've never seen one as perfect as that one. They all have smudges or have crinkled edges. That document was supposed to be in a drawer for sixteen years but it looked like they printed it yesterday."

"Hmm. You have a point."

Christine stuffed the papers in the folder and put them in the file cabinet. "I'm going to look into this."

Niles followed Alyce around that first day. She introduced him as her twin brother to everyone she went to. One girl, Darcy, came up to her and hugged her. "You have a twin brother? How come you never told me?" She gave Niles a hug. "Wow, you're so strong."

He shook his head. *Why did she say that?* "Thanks," he mumbled.

Three boys came up to Niles. "Why were you hugging Darcy?"

"She hugged me, honest."

"You didn't seem to mind. I'll meet you outside in the schoolyard during lunch."

Niles shrugged. "Why don't you just talk to me now."

"He's a real smarty, punch him now, Sam."

Sam took a swing at him, but Niles easily dodged it. "I don't want a fight."

"Well, you got one." Sam took another swing at him but missed. Niles hit him in the chest. Sam went backward into the far wall and then hit the floor.

"I'm sorry. I didn't mean to hurt you but you kept trying to hit me."

Two teachers ran into the middle of the now-gathered crowd. "Break it up. You two are coming with me to the principal's office."

"I didn't mean to hurt him," Niles said.

Sam moaned. "I can't get up."

"Get the school nurse," the one teacher told the other.

Soon the nurse came running.

"It's bad. He's going to need X-rays. Call an ambulance."

Niles found himself sitting in front of the principal. She glared at him. "What did you do to that student?"

"I only kept him from hitting me."

"This is your first day of class and already you're attacking your fellow students. What is your problem?" Niles decided not to answer. She glared harder. "Are you really Alyce's brother? Your birth certificate was a lot less tattered than hers." He still held his tongue. "I want answers, young man," she yelled.

George stepped into the room. "The secretary called me in. What is the meaning of this?"

She pointed at Niles. "He sent another child to the hospital."

"Did you get the whole story? Because what I heard from Alyce and Darcy is that Sam swung at Niles twice before Niles defended himself," George bellowed back.

Sam's dad rushed into the room. "I want this child arrested for assault. He hurt my son."

Niles sat there not responding to anyone. He didn't know how arguments were supposed to go on Earth. They seemed very similar to Valderon, but he wanted to make sure.

"I'll call the police and then I'll expel him from the school. We don't need troublemakers like him." Christine picked up the phone.

"You're not listening to the facts," George protested.

Just then Sam and his mother walked into the room. "Ribs are bruised but not broken. Man, you have a mean right hook, Niles. It felt like being hit by a ton of bricks."

"This isn't funny," Sam's dad yelled.

Sam smiled. "It is. I swung at Niles twice before he responded. It was totally my fault."

"What did I tell you about not starting a fight you can't finish?" Sam's dad asked.

"Is that how you are raising your child?" Christine stood up. "I think we have all learned a lesson here. Sam got his just rewards. Niles, I'm watching you. If any other children end up hurt, I don't care who starts it, you will be punished. Now all of you, get out of my office." She pointed at the door.

Chapter Ten
Math Class

George drove the twins home. Niles headed out into the forest behind the house and sat there for the longest time. He listened to the birds singing and watched the sun go down. He gazed at all the trees in turn and felt the dirt beneath the pine needles. *What am I doing here? I don't belong here.* A few minutes later the three dogs came running up to him and sat down around him. "You like me now? You tried to eat me when I first arrived."

Alyce came out an hour later and sat down beside him. "Are you still upset about the fight you got into?"

"I didn't do anything. He kept swinging at me. I didn't ask Darcy to come up and hug me. I didn't know she was his girlfriend."

Alyce shook her head. "She isn't. She can't stand him. I think you made her happy when you knocked him across the room. She really likes you, by the way."

"She doesn't know me. My heart is on the other side of my chest. She's going to figure that out eventually. I think I avoid all human entanglements for the time being."

"But not with us, right?"

"Of course not."

Alyce stood up. "Come back to the house. Dinner is almost ready."

As they made their way into the house his mom set the food on the table. "Oh, there you are. I heard there were problems at school today. Are you okay?"

"Yes, I am fine." He sat down next to his new dad. They said grace and then he dished himself a portion as they passed it around."

"Have you ever had lasagna before?"

"No, but it's red and that is supposed to be good." He took a forkful. "It is good."

"Thank you," Janice replied.

As everyone ate, the conversation lagged. Niles gazed around the room. He had never been so included. With his father, he sat down at the foot of a long table, so long it wasn't conducive to the conversation. The servants would bring round and round of food, too much food. He would only pick out a few items of what he liked best. He often wondered what ever happened to the leftovers. There were always lots of leftovers. Not in this family, though. Leftovers were not a thing.

After dinner, Alyce said, "It's the twins' turn to do the dishes."

"Okay." Niles shrugged. "What am I supposed to do?"

Alyce's mouth gaped open. "You have never done dishes?"

"No."

"Who did the dishes in your house?"

"The servants."

"You had servants? Wow. How many servants did you have?"

"I think there were twenty. I never counted them."

"You don't know? Did you even know their names?"

"Most of them. The cooks, I didn't ever interact with. They were always in the kitchen. I never went in there."

"Okay." Alyce took a deep breath. "You run the water until it's hot, but not hot enough to burn your hands. Then you put the soap in. I like lots of bubbles so I put more than Mom does. Then you put in each pan and scrub them until they're clean. You will hand them to me and I will rinse them."

"I didn't know the servants had to do all this."

"It's not even all of it. Lucia is loading the dishwasher. These are the pots and pans only."

Niles cleared his throat. "Wow." He scrubbed each dish in turn and then gave it to Alyce to rinse. She would hand it back if he missed a spot so he became better at getting all the edges the first time.

When they were done, she said, "See, that wasn't so bad."

"I'm thinking about my father's servants now. I think we paid them too much."

She slapped his arm. "You're such a tease." She walked away.

I wasn't teasing, he sighed. *Oh, well. They are most likely working for someone else by now.*

That night Niles stared at the ceiling of his new room. The almost-fight upset him more than he could say and then the principal seemed to have it in for him for some reason. If Sam hadn't come back when he did, Niles would have been expelled. Every time Niles closed his eyes he saw Sam flying across the hallway into the far wall. *How did I do that?*

After a nearly sleepless night, Niles woke up and dressed. After breakfast he headed for the bus. When he arrived at school, the secretary met him in the entryway. "This is your class schedule."

He gave it a quick look. "I don't have any classes with my sister."

"I'm sorry." She leaned in. "The principal has it in for you, be careful."

He nodded and then headed off to his first class. The math teacher had thick, dark-rimmed glasses. He nodded when Niles walked into the room. "Take a seat, young Niles. Welcome to Timberlake High School."

Sam waved at him. "Over here." Niles walked over and sat at a desk next to him. "I thought you hated me after I hurt you."

"Nah, it was all my fault."

"Ahem." The teacher said. "Young Niles, you missed the test yesterday. I'm going to give you an assignment to do while I go and grade it. I want you to add all the numbers from one to one hundred together. The first person to finish will get ten points extra credit." Niles raised his hand. "Yes, young Niles, do you have a question?"

"No, I have the answer. It's 5050."

The teacher's jaw dropped open. "Have you done this before, perhaps?"

"No, it's easy. You add 100 plus 1 and you get 101. You add 2 plus 99 and you get 101, you add 3 plus 98 and you get 101, and so on. All you have to do is times 101 by 50 and you get 5050."

The teacher folded his arms. "There's more to you than meets the eye. I'm impressed."

Chapter Eleven
Problems with the Birth Certificate

Christine had copies of Alyce's and Niles' birth certificates side by side. "What do you think, Albert? You deal with records more than I do."

Albert, the president of the school board scratched his chin. "There is a problem with Niles' birth certificate. You see the two-digit number on the record ID is supposed to be the two-digit year and then a string of numbers unique to this record. They say 04 but Niles shows that he was born in 2008 according to the record down here. This record has been altered."

"I see. There is no way that child is twenty years old. I'm calling the mom."

Janise's heart skipped a beat when she saw the call from the school. "Oh, no. Not again." She answered it in her most pleasant voice. "Hello."

"Mrs. Morgan, your son's birth certificate has been altered. I think he's an imposter trying to take advantage of you."

Janise giggled. "I'm so glad it wasn't something more serious. I was worried after yesterday. He's my son, I'm a hundred percent sure of that. It's probably a clerical error with the county. I'll get it straighten out. These things happen all the time, I hear."

"I don't think that's it," Christine protested.

"No, it is. He passed all the tests. He's my son. Sorry, I have to go." Janice hung up the phone. She pulled out Niles' birth certificate again. Oh, the two-digit date. That's the problem. Calling up Lucia, she said, "Can you have your friend fix the two-digit date on the document number to match the year date?"

"Yes, I can do that."

"Oh, and does he have a way to age the document so it looks sixteen years old?"

"He's very good with that stuff."

"I don't want to know why you know that, but thanks."

"Oh, thank you for not asking."

When Niles dressed for P.E. he ran out to the track where the assistant coaches waited for him. "We want to see how fast you run. We will time you on the sixty-yard dash. Go ahead and stretch so you won't pull a muscle."

Sam ran up to them. "Do you mind if I watch?"

Coach shrugged, "No problem."

"I'm ready," Niles said. "What's a sixty-yard dash?"

The assistant coach pointed. "You run from this line to that line and we time you."

"Okay."

The coach trotted down to the finish line. "Ready, set, go." Niles ran as fast as he could.

When the coach made it back to the start line he showed his assistant the time. "6.5. That would be a school record. I must have timed that wrong. Why don't you time this one?" The assistant made his way to the finish line. "Niles, I'm going to have you run that again. I think there was something wrong with my stopwatch."

"Sure."

The assistant held his arm up in the air. "On your mark, get set, go." Niles ran it again.

When the assistant arrived back he motioned the coach over to the side. "You're right, we did get different times." He held his stopwatch up. "6.4."

"Wow, that kid is fast." They both walked over to Sam and Niles. "Did you ever give any thought to trying out for the track team?"

Niles shook his head. "What's a track team?"

"How did he do?" Sam asked. "Like the best ever?"

"Something like that," the coach replied.

"I knew it." Sam walked away smiling.

Between classes, Niles sneaked between two shelves at the library, not noticing Darcy following him. He pushed the button on his watch. "Gina, why am I so much stronger than these humans?"

"The gravitational pull on Valderon is stronger than that of Earth's. You should hide your true strength from now on."

"Oh, thanks."

She went on. "I need to recharge because I'm spending too much time in the trees on your mom's property. Can you take me out into space soon so I can get close to the sun?"

"Yes, of course."

Darcy backed up and walked out of the library, then ran down the hall. Out of breath when she found Alyce, she said. "Alyce, you are in danger. I think Niles is an alien."

"Shhh." Alyce put her finger to her lips. Then she gave Darcy her innocent smile. "Why would you think that?" She blinked twice.

"He just talked into his watch and the watch said he was from a place called Valderon."

"Oh, I'm sure there is a perfectly good explanation for that."

Darcy folded her arms. "And that would be?"

"I can't think of anything off the top of my head." Alyce lowered her voice. "Please don't tell anyone."

Taking a step back, Darcy clutched her chest. "What?"

Alyce took her arm and led her to a quiet spot. "Please. I'm not in danger. He is my brother, but not my twin. He's a great guy and wouldn't hurt a flea."

"Except for Sam?"

"Okay, I forgot about Sam, but Sam deserved it."

Darcy nodded. "Okay, I won't tell a soul, but I want the whole story."

"Not today, I have to get to class." Alyce hurried off.

Chapter Twelve
Expelled

At the end of the day, Christine sent the secretary to pull Niles out of his last class. When he sat down in front of her, he didn't say a word. "I guess you're wondering why I called you in here." He still held his tongue. "Very well, I'll get straight to the point. I'm expelling you. I think your birth certificate has been changed and I think you're a fraud impersonating a mother's long-lost boy. That is a terrible thing to do. What do you have to say for yourself?" He still didn't say anything. She glared. "Goodbye then."

Walking out, he ran into Sam. "Are you in trouble again for hitting me?"

"Not for that. She accused me of being a fraud and expelled me."

Sam looked at him for a minute. "I don't think she can do that."

"She did."

"Okay, I think we all deserve a day off." He pulled out his phone and made a call and then another.

Niles climbed on the bus, but then Alyce stuck her head through the door. "Mom's going to drive us home."

"Thanks." He walked back off and then went into the car.

"How did your day go at school?"

"In math class, the teacher raved about how smart Niles is," Alyce beamed.

"That's nice. How about you, Niles?"

"I got expelled."

"What? Why?"

"The principal says I'm a fraud and impersonating your long-lost son. She thinks I'm a terrible person because of it."

"I'll show her. Lucia said the birth certificate is done and done right this time. They are even aging the paper. It will be tomorrow after school though."

"A day off sounds good. I have to recharge Gina's battery anyway. I'll head up after dinner."

"How do you recharge her batteries?" Alyce asked.

"I have to fly her up close to the sun."

She gave him a broad smile. "Can I go with you?"

"I don't see why not."

She clapped her hands and jumped up and down. "Yeah!"

The next morning, the bus stopped at the normal spot, but there were no students to pick up. The driver opened the door and stepped out. She scanned up and down the road. Climbing back in, she waited five minutes and then drove to the next stop. The same thing happened again. After finishing her route, she pulled up to the school with one girl sitting in the back.

The girl looked at the two empty school buses next to her. "I don't want to be the only one in school today, I'm going to

call my mom and tell her to come get me."
She hopped off the bus with her phone in
her hand.

The math teacher and P.E. coach
marched into Christine's office. "What were
you thinking?" the coach asked.

"She obviously wasn't thinking," the
math teacher said. "She expelled the
brightest and strongest kid in school for a
reason that isn't covered in the school
charter."

"He's a fraud," Christine replied.
"Don't you have classes to teach?"

"Nobody told you, I bet. But there
are a total of six kids in school today and
most of those are going home or thinking
about it," Coach said.

"What?" Christine rushed into the
hall and went classroom by classroom.
Teachers were sitting at their desks facing
empty classrooms.

The coach had followed her out.
"They posted on Facebook and all the social
media sites. They won't be back until you
let Niles back."

"I'll expel them all!" she snarled.

He shook his head. "Then we all lose our jobs. Without students, they don't need us."

She stomped back into her office right past a woman standing near the back. "Oh Ms. Iverson, I didn't see you."

Ms. Iverson folded her arms. "I just came from an emergency school board meeting. We caught wind of what was happening. I have to tell you, your job is hanging by a thread. You get that student, and all the rest of them, back here now."

A man stepped in a minute later. "I'm Justin Albright, attorney at law. I represent the Morgan family. Here is, what I believe, is the original birth certificate. One of their daughters was playing with a photo program and created the other one as a joke. Janice Morgan brought the wrong one to you. I'm also notifying you that if Niles isn't back in school by tomorrow, the family will sue the school district."

Ms. Iverson took the birth certificate. "This looks genuine to me. I assure you the school district does not want to get sued over this minor misunderstanding. Niles will be in school tomorrow, won't he, Christine?" She didn't give Christine the birth certificate but gave it to the secretary who put it right in the file.

"Um, yes." Christine sighed.

"I'll be on my way then." Justin turned on his heels and marched out like he had marched in.

"I guess you will be sending an apology letter to the Morgan family and you will write it personally. I don't want the secretary drafting it for you." She pointed at Christine. "Understood?"

"Yes," Christine snarled under her breath.

"Good. It sounds like this has been resolved. I'll just be on my way then." Ms. Iverson left.

Chapter Thirteen
A Trip Toward the Sun

Alyce bounced in her seat at the breakfast table. Her ear-to-ear smile and giddy giggling irritated Lucia. "Stop already."

"I can't. I get to go up in space today."

Niles ate his cold cereal with a smile seeing her so happy. When he finished, he put down his spoon. "It's time."

Alyce jumped up from the table but her mother said, "You need to finish your breakfast."

Shaking her head, Alyce smiled. "Too excited." She followed Niles out of the house and into the back.

To Niles' surprise, the whole family followed the two of them into the woods.

"Gina, decloak."

"Are you sure this is safe?" George finally asked. "I don't want to lose either one of you."

"Yes. I flew across the galaxy in it and through the solar system with it leaking oxygen. This is only a half day there and back again and the air leak is fixed. Thanks again."

"Can you take all of us?" Janice asked.

"I only have two seats, sorry."

"There is a jump seat under the stasis chamber that bolts into the floor," Gina said out of the blue.

Niles shrugged. "Okay, I can take one more. Who wants to go?"

Janice and Lucia shook their heads. "I guess I get to then." George's face broke out into a smile.

"Honey, let the twins have their fun," Janice rubbed George's back.

He sighed but nodded.

Niles and Alyce sat down in the seats and strapped themselves in. Niles hit some buttons, but a loud squawk came out of the console. They both jumped. It flashed red. "Password required."

He scowled up at the monitor. "It's me, Niles."

"That will work. Go ahead with manual controls. The yokes are in the drawers under the console," Gina replied.

They each pulled out what looked like a bowtie steering wheel and put them into round holes on the edge of the console. They clicked into place. Niles pulled up on the yoke and the ship lifted up between the trees knocking off some pine needles as it went.

"Do you actually know how to fly this thing?" Alyce seemed suddenly nervous.

"Now you ask?" Gina fussed.

"We have computer games that mimic flight and control of this type of spaceship and many more," Niles reassured her. He gazed over at her white face and hands clutching onto the console. She didn't seem reassured.

As he pulled the yoke up steeper, they traveled past the clouds and headed toward the stars.

"Dimming viewscreen, head toward the sun," Gina said.

Niles turned hard to port. The sun stood directly in their path. He pushed the throttle forward and soon they were moving faster and faster.

Alyce gasped and then said, "Wow."

The ship went up and up until finally, Gina said, "This is far enough. We are past the Earth's atmosphere. I can recharge just fine here."

Alyce took off her seatbelt. "Why am I not floating like the astronauts do?"

"Artificial gravity," Niles replied.

"I want to float." She gave him a big smile.

"Gina, turn off the artificial gravity."

They both floated up. "Wow." She moved around until she made it back next to the engine. "Is this the stasis chamber?"

"I spent two years in there. Gina tricked me into laying down."

"I'm getting a little nauseated."

"Turning back on artificial gravity," Gina said.

"Slowly, please. I don't want to smack into the floor."

They drifted down until they gained their feet. "That was fun. Can we fly around the moon now?"

"Um."

"Fully recharged," Gina said. "Take us there."

"All right." They strapped themselves in and he took the yoke, then pushed the throttle forward. "Next stop the moon." He thought for a minute. "Gina, what is the real name of the moon?"

"It's just called the moon."

He cleared his throat. "How about we call it Alyce's Moon."

"Updating star charts."

"Really! That's so awesome." Alyce bounced up and down in her seat.

The moon took longer to get to than the edge of the atmosphere but soon they were orbiting it. Niles pointed out features and Gina told them what each one of the features was. He buzzed down across the Sea of Tranquility and then back up to the light side of the moon before heading back home.

Chapter Fourteen
Caught

Sam caught a ride over to the Morgan's house. He had a goal of making Niles his friend and 'ditch day' was the perfect opportunity. When he rang the bell, no one answered. The dogs didn't even bark and he thought it was odd. He thought he heard talking in the back yard so he went back into the woods. When he found them, the family and the dogs stood gazing up at something. A minute later the spaceship landed and Niles stepped out.

When Alyce followed she jumped up and down. "We got to go around the moon. It was so much fun."

"Sam?" Niles said. The whole family turned. He stood there wide-eyed as the dogs milled around him. "Sam, what are you doing here?"

Sam stood there, but no answers came.

Janice patted George's shoulder. "Honey, take him into the house with us. He seems upset."

They all sat down in the living room. Sam finally caught his breath. "That was a sp— spaceship."

"It's more like a helicopter without rotors," Lucia shot back.

Sam shook his head and pointed at Alyce. "She said they went around the moon. That's in space."

"It was so awesome!" Alyce held her hands to her chest.

"See." Sam gazed over at Lucia.

"What were you doing here anyway?" Niles asked.

"I want to be your friend. I know I upset you the first day of school by trying to hit you."

"Twice," Niles added.

"Okay, I tried to hit you twice. I was jealous that Darcy would hug you when she's never hugged me. I like her but she doesn't like me. I'm over that. I think you're a great guy." He paused. "And now I see you have a spaceship. How cool is that?"

George looked him in the eye. "You can't tell anyone what you saw today."

"I won't. I promise."

Janice picked up her phone when it rang. After excusing herself from the conversation, she walked down the hall and then came back a minute later. "The school has reconsidered. They aren't expelling Niles after all."

"That's good news," Niles replied.

"I guess I'll call off the ditch days," Sam stood up. "I have to get home."

"Wait," Niles stood. "You organized the ditch day?"

"Yes. The principal didn't have a right to expel you." Sam waved as he headed out the door.

"Bye." Alyce waved at a closed door.

The next day at school, Niles tried to avoid both Sam and the principal. It didn't work out as the principal walked past him in the hall and glared. Sam sat by him in math class. When the teacher had his back turned he whispered, "That spacecraft of yours is really something."

Niles made sure no one around him heard. What he didn't expect was Darcy coming up to his locker and standing there. "Um, hello."

"What are you?" she demanded. "You know what I mean."

He shrugged, stalling for time.

"I heard your phone tell you that on your planet the gravity was higher so you were stronger than earthlings."

"Were you spying on me?" He asked.

"No, of course not. Well, actually, I was. I thought you were kinda cute, but then your watch said you were like from another planet."

"I assure you that Janice Morgan is my mother and that Alyce is in fact, my sister."

"What about what your watch said?"

"Watches don't always tell the truth. Sometimes they don't even tell time correctly."

"I resent that," Gina said.

"Not now, Gina."

"Oh, it has a name. None of my watches ever had a name." Darcy thought for a minute. "Except for my Micky Mouse watch when I was a kid, but that doesn't count. I never had a watch that I could have conversations with."

"I have to get to class. I'll talk to you later, Okay."

She scowled and then walked off.

This is harder than it needs to be. When I lived on a Valderon, no one had a problem that I was born on another planet and that I was half-alien. These Earthlings. How can they possibly think they are alone in the galaxy? He shook his head as he walked toward science class.

The science teacher had rolled in an oversized television on a cart into the room. "Can anyone tell me what happened in space yesterday that caused such an uproar in the news?"

One of the students raised her hand. "Yes, there was a strange spot on the moon."

"That's exactly right. It was not only a spot, but it was shaped like a minivan with skids on the bottom. Here is a close-up of it taken by the Moana Loa Observatory in Hawaii. You see it's a square shape and has what appears to be windows in it. It's silhouetted against the bright side of the moon in this picture. It circled the moon and then disappeared behind it. Can anyone suggest what this might have been?"

Niles' jaw dropped open. *Oh no!*

Chapter Fifteen
Darcy's Suspicions

On his way to the bus after school, he met up with Alyce. "They saw us," she said.

"I know. Let's get home quickly."

They walked around the corner and came face to face with Darcy. She had her hands on her hips. "What's going on? You two have been so evasive every time I try to talk to you. I want answers. Especially now that there are spaceships between us and the moon. Is Earth going to be invaded? Should I panic?"

"No, don't worry," Alyce replied. "That was just us. You'll be fine."

"What?" Darcy's face turned red.

"I wish you wouldn't have said that." He grabbed Darcy's arm. "Come home with us. I guess you'll want some answers. I'll have Mom or Lucia drive you home afterward. We'll explain things when we get there."

She put her hand over her heart. "Okay." After inhaling a few deep breaths, she replied, "I *would* like some answers." She followed them onto the bus and then phoned her mom. When she hung up she said, "My mom will pick me up in an hour. After you tell me what's going on."

"Okay, great," Alyce smiled.

Niles leaned back in his chair. He watched the scenery go by. He wondered where his father was and what he was up to. Life wasn't so complicated back on Valderon. He didn't even have to get dressed by himself. His valet helped with that. The servants cared for his every need. Now he had to hide who he was but they were figuring it out anyway.

When the bus stopped, the three of them piled out. They headed into the house where Janice had just put a roast in the crockpot. "Hi, Darcy." She gazed over at Niles and Alyce.

"She wants answers," Alyce said.

"Your mother knows, too." Darcy folded her arms. "First I hear Niles talking on his phone asking why he's so much stronger than Earthlings. When I ask Alyce about it, she's tight-lipped. Then there is a strange craft hovering over the Earth somewhere. Alyce tells me not to worry because it was Niles and her flying around. How is that even possible?"

"I see." Janice gave questioning glances at Niles and Alyce again. "Who else have you told about all this?"

"No one. Alyce said to be quiet and not tell anyone."

"That's good. It seems like you two need to be more careful." She scowled at the twins.

"She followed me into the library when I talked to Gina. I didn't even know she was there," Niles replied.

Janice was about to ask why, but Darcy blushed, so she figured it out. "Okay, damage control here. Sam and now Darcy."

Niles shook his head. "Sam won't talk."

Alyce added, "Darcy won't either. Will you?"

"I won't. Just tell me what's going on. I was awake all night worried about alien invasions."

Alyce piped up. "He has a spaceship. It is so much fun. We flew out around the moon. That's where the observatory spotted us I guess. We won't be doing that again."

"So, there are no aliens?" Darcy asked.

"Well, just a half of one." Niles raised his hand.

"A half of one. How are you half-alien when you're a twin?"

"He isn't my actual twin," Alyce admitted. "It's just that he spent four years in stasis and you don't age while you're in stasis, so he's my age and it didn't make sense to be around my age when he's actually two years older than my sister. His father was my mom's first husband. She didn't know he was an alien until Niles was born with his heart on the right side. Rather than trying to explain that, his dad kidnapped Niles and took him to his home planet, but now Niles is back." She stopped to draw a breath. "Does any of this make any sense?"

"Not really." Darcy stepped toward Niles. "Can I feel for your heart?"

He shrugged. "Sure."

She felt around longer than Niles thought she needed to, but she finally said. "Wow. That's so cool," and then gave him a hug.

Over her shoulder, he mouthed, "Help me," until she released the hug.

Darcy checked her phone. "Well, my mom is here. I have to go." She waved to Janice and Alyce but gave Niles a smile and a wink.

Janice smiled at him. "Did you have a girlfriend on your old planet? Because it looks like you have one here."

"She keeps hugging me." He shivered. "I have homework, I'm going to my room."

"I can help you with dinner," Alyce smiled.

"Is it just me or is Darcy chasing Niles?"

"Now, she totally has the hots for him. I thought she would give it a pause when she found out he was half alien, but her eyes lit up when she found out. Did you see how long she checked his chest out? It was much longer than she needed to."

"I did notice that."

Niles opened his books, but it only took him fifteen minutes to do his homework. He knew all the answers as soon as he read the questions. A private tutor for his whole life on Valderon was now a problem. He was bored with school. He wanted to avoid Sam and Darcy. Sam was too much into his business and Darcy was too much into him. He leaned back. He thought of his home and his life. This life wasn't bad, but it was harder for him to control. He could order his servants around, but couldn't do the same thing with his family.

He loved his family more than he had ever gotten attached to his father or the

household staff. *What do I do about Darcy?*
He didn't know. After an hour, Janice called
the family together for dinner. He would
spend the rest of the day and into the night
absorbed in his own thoughts.

Chapter Sixteen
Sam the Sidekick

The school wasn't interesting anymore. The math teacher would put a problem on the board and then ask Niles if he knew the answer. When Niles said yes, the teacher would smile. "I'll put a harder one up then." He then ask Niles again. When he found one Niles couldn't answer off the top of his head, the teacher would announce that problem as a pop quiz.

The other students were getting upset because the questions were so hard they couldn't solve most of them. They would glare at Niles. Sam leaned over to him, "Just say no, you can't solve it. Cut us some slack."

Niles sighed. A minute later his phone went off, so he rushed into the hall to figure out what Gina wanted.

"There is a probe entering the Niles' Solar System. It's a DNA recognition probe. I fear they have followed me. Get home quick. We need to intercept it. I think it's looking for your father, but it will spot you too and then they will send a warship to take you back and throw you in prison."

"I'm on my way." Niles turned to see Sam standing behind him.

"Let's go," Sam said.

"No, this is my problem and mine only."

"I'm your sidekick. I'm in this too. Come on, you can ride on the back of my motor scooter. It'll be a lot faster than running." They arrived at the scooter and Sam put on his helmet. "Sorry, I don't have one for you."

Niles climbed on the back. It wasn't long before he was hanging on for dear life. He had never been on a scooter before so he didn't know what to do. After a few bumps that nearly knocked him off the back, he put his arms around Sam, figuring that if he was going to fall off, he would pull Sam off with him. He didn't like how it leaned around the corners. When they hit highway forty-one, Sam increased speed. With his hair flapping in the breeze, Niles closed his eyes to the oncoming wind. Finally, they hit the road up the hill to Niles' house.

He stood up, shaking.

"What did you think? I bet you could talk your parents into getting one of these also. They are not that expensive."

Niles shook his head. "I will never ride on one of those again as long as I live."

"Oh, it was fun, you just don't realize it. Let's get to your ship."

They headed into the backyard. Gina had already decloaked at their approach. They stepped in and sat down. "Strap yourself in," Niles said.

"Who is this?" Gina's monitor clicked to life.

"I'm Sam. I'm Niles' sidekick."

"Oh, good. I have a watch for you so I can communicate when Niles is out of town."

"Don't give him a watch," Niles protested.

"He's your sidekick." The drawer under the monitor popped open. Sam took out the watch.

"Thank you." He strapped it on.

"You are more than welcome, Sam. Before we leave, I need you two to search the hull for a tracer. It's a little black disk against my hull somewhere that is the shape of an American quarter, only a lot thicker."

They both piled out. Searching high, Niles couldn't find anything, but Sam found it close to the exhaust port of the starboard engine. "Got it." He picked up a rock.

"Don't destroy it. Put it on the side of the skid. I can demagnetize that when we are in space. It will float around and they will never again figure out where it's leading them."

"Okay." Sam stuck it on the skid. They piled back into the spaceship. "How do you fly this thing?" He put his hand on the yoke.

"You don't," Niles answered. "In fact, don't touch anything. We have a non-friction bubble surrounding us when we leave the atmosphere and when we return to it. If you move the yoke too fast during that time you can, well, burst our bubble and we will burn up in the atmosphere."

"Okay then," Sam pulled his hands back rapidly and held them up in the air. He carefully set them in his lap. "Let's do this." Niles hit the button and they slowly rose up through the trees and into the sky, going higher and higher. Sam gazed out the window and gasped. As they went higher he gazed down at the Earth below him. "This is getting real."

They headed towards the dark side of the moon. Niles didn't want to get silhouetted against it again. He flew down close to the surface. "Okay, now, Gina."

"Skids demagnetized, tracking is falling fast." Gaining altitude, they hid behind the moon waiting to see what happened. "It didn't work. It's going toward the only inhabited planet in the solar system. It will scan toward the Earth. As long as we stay behind it, it won't spot you."

Niles turned toward the monitor. "We're supposed to sit out here in space indefinitely?"

"The battery on the probe lasts only about ten years."

Niles sat back in his chair and folded his arms. "This is all my father's fault."

"Teach me how to fly this thing," Sam said.

"Why would I teach you how to fly it?"

Sam held up his watch. "I'm the sidekick."

Niles' eyes narrowed. "Fine. The yoke is in front of you. Steer it like a car. The directional counters are on your right. That's how you know where you're going. It's up and down for the one, port and starboard for the other. The throttle is at your left hand. That controls the speed."

Sam smiled. "Tell me where the probe is located, Gina. I want to see it."

"Steer 15226 horizon and 25982 vertical and you'll run right into it."

Sam pushed the throttle forward as he watched the counters. When he had them pointed toward where Gina told him, he held that position as he headed through space. When he saw the small probe up ahead, he pushed the thruster all the way forward.

"What are you doing?" Niles gasped.

The ship hit the probe with a thud and then it split into a thousand different pieces. Sam pulled back on the throttle. "End of problem."

Chapter Seventeen
Father's Message

"I can't believe you did that," Niles snarled at Sam.

"Listen, you couldn't come back down to Earth until that probe was gone, so I was stuck up there too because we're in this ship together. I have a social studies test tomorrow. I need to get back home. Besides, I'm your sidekick, remember?"

"How can I forget? You keep reminding me."

"Anyway, I solved the problem. You're welcome."

"They're just going to send another probe."

Gina interjected, "Another probe sent from Valderon would take two years and five months to reach Earth if they decided to send it in the first place. They are looking for your father, not you, but if they find you, they will arrest you."

"Thanks, Gina." Niles sighed, "And thank you, too, Sam."

"You're welcome."

As they came into the Earth's atmosphere, Niles' father's face came on the monitor. "I want my ship back. It's supposed to be on the way back to me, but I see that it isn't." He folded his arms and glared.

"Hello, Dad. It's good to see you too." Niles' voice dripped with sarcasm.

"I'm not happy. What did you do, overwrite the programmed for the return trip?"

"You're not getting your ship back, is what it boils down to. You kidnapped me from my mother and then kicked me out of the only home I remember. I now live in a world I'm having to adjust to. No, I might need this ship again. Do you know it had a tracker placed on it? A probe from Valderon came looking for you."

They watched Craig's face redden. "I've been betrayed. Only my inner circle knew about that ship. Someone has given me away." He scratched his chin. "I don't even know what to think about this. Keep the ship. It's now a hindrance to me. I'm going to have to check the ship I'm on for trackers now. I may just be one small step ahead of being found." Pacing back and forth he finally stopped. "If I sent a probe with a data pad on it, do you think you can put your thumbprint to it? James forgot to do that account when he did the others."

"No. If there is money out there in my name, I'm keeping it."

"What do you need galactic credits for? You can't spend them on Earth. They are not part of the universal monetary system."

"I might not stay on Earth. Who knows where I'll end up?"

"You have to stay," Sam said.

Craig turned to him. "Who are you?"

"I'm Niles' sidekick."

"You have a sidekick?"

Niles folded his arms. "Yes, I do. What business is that of yours?"

"I'm your father."

"And such a father you turned out to be." Gina cut the feed." Craig's face disappeared from the monitor. "What account is he talking about?"

"Account with Felgado credit has one million two hundred and three thousand credits in it. It is in your name."

"Wow," Sam said. "Is that a lot?"

Gina replied. "One credit is worth roughly one hundred twenty-three Earth dollars. It's an approximate because there isn't a direct exchange with Earth."

"Wow, that's um..." Sam put a finger up to his cheek. "Um..."

"One hundred forty-seven million nine hundred sixty-nine thousand," Niles replied.

"I was just about to say that."

They set down gently and exited the ship. Gina turned into an old wood shed again and the two of them headed toward the house. Dusk had come by then. Sam hopped on his scooter and said goodbye as he drove off. Niles headed into the house.

"Where have you been?" Janice asked. "Everyone has eaten. I was also told by that principal who wants you gone, that you left school early."

"I had an emergency in space. There was a probe looking for me. We destroyed it."

"A probe?" She shook her head. "How often is this going to happen that they have probes looking for you?"

"It will take years for them to send another one so I'll be safe for a while."

She pulled out his dinner out of the fridge and put it into the microwave. "Who's we?"

"Sam and me. He's the one who ran the ship into the probe and destroyed it. He's my self-appointed sidekick."

She set his plate on the table and then scooped up some ice cream and sat down with him and ate it. "Do you like Sam?"

"I guess so. He seems to like me."

"How about Darcy?"

"She scares me. She's coming on too strong."

She giggled. "I saw that."

Alyce came into the kitchen. "There you are. I thought you went back to where you came from when you and Gina were both gone."

"I had an emergency in space."

"I'm glad you're back." She hugged him.

Chapter Eighteen
Back in School

The teacher frowned when Sam and Niles walked into math class. "Where did you two go?"

"Niles had an emergency. I went to help him," Sam said before Niles could answer.

"You helped?" the teacher asked.

"He was a good help." Niles came to his defense.

"Next time you have an emergency, a parent needs to call the office and I would find someone other than Sam to help you. He needs to stay in class. He needs all the math help he can get."

"Yes, Sir," Niles said.

After class when Niles went to his locker to put his books away, Darcy came up to him and put her hand on the right side of his chest. "I just love feeling your heartbeat."

"Stop it." He snarled. "You're going to make everyone think I'm a freak."

She pulled her hand back. "Sorry." She gave him a dazzling smile. "I hope you're not mad at me."

"No. Just don't give me away."

"Oh, no. I like my little alien," she whispered in his ear then kissed his cheek.

He rolled his eyes where she couldn't see. As he headed towards the bus, Niles came across Sam. "Do you need help with math?"

Sam looked up and down the hall like it was a big secret. "I might not pass. If I flunk math, I'll have to take tenth grade over again."

"We can't let that happen. Call your mom and tell her you're coming to my house tonight. Bring your math book."

"Okay. Do you want to ride on my scooter again?"

"No, I value my life. I'll take the bus."

As they sat around the kitchen table, Niles kept going over the problems.

"How can the answer be five? I subtract one from times and then times it by three. The answer should be three." Sam said.

"No, you have to times and divide before you add and subtract, so this one is a trick question. Minus one plus two times three. The answer is 5. Two times three is six minus one is five."

"Oh." Sam stared at the problem again. "Oh. I get it."

"Good, now let's start on the graphs."

Sam leaned back. "How did you get to be so good at math? Did you do the same math on your planet?"

"Math is universal. There are different names for the equations, but it's the same math. The math we are doing now Valderonian kids do in their sixth year of school. Although I didn't go to school. I had private tutors, so I was way ahead of the schoolchildren. When you use math to guide ships across the galaxy, even a small error of a fraction of a percent can leave you light-years away from your destination. You have to learn it early and very well when you're a space-going race. You don't have room for error."

"So, all this is review for you?"

"Yes, very boring review. It's nice that you let me tutor you. It makes it more interesting."

Alyce walked into the kitchen, opened her math book, and sat down at the table. "I overheard you. I want to learn math better too."

"Great." Niles smiled. "Now we are going to graphs."

Janice invited Sam to dinner that night. It was late when he headed home on his scooter. Janice worried about sending him home in the dark. "I should have made him stay," she finally said out loud.

"I'll follow him in Gina," Niles volunteered.

"I'll go with him," Alyce said.

Niles thought to himself that she didn't really need to be there, but maybe an extra set of eyes would be good.

"Yes, you two, hurry," Janice urged.

They ran into the backyard and hopped in Gina. "Can you track Sam?" Niles asked.

"He has the watch. I can track him easily." She took off into the night. Soon they were hovering over Sam as he drove along with Gina turning off all of her exterior lights. "That truck has run the last two stop signs and is on a trajectory to hit Sam at this next intersection."

"What can we do?" Alyce asked.

Gina came in behind the truck and sent a blue light onto it then stopped. The truck also came to a screeching halt. A minute later, she turned off the light. "Sam has cleared the intersection. He's safe now."

"Thank you, Gina."

They floated up. The man in the truck staggered to the back of it and scanned all the tires. He shrugged and then began to stagger back towards the cab. Just then a sheriff's deputy pulled in behind and turned on his lights. "That was lucky, a cop showed up right then," Niles said.

"No luck involved. I called them."

"You can call 911?"

"How do you think I contact you on your watch?"

"I guess I never thought about it."

"Sam is home now and we are headed towards yours."

"Thank you, Gina," both Alyce and Niles said.

Chapter Nineteen
Warship

In science class, the teacher put another picture of the moon up. "This time it looks as if there is another UFO between us and the moon. This one has things sticking out of it and the nose is pointier than the last one. Someone has criticized the Moana Loa Observatory of having a bug on its lens, an accusation that they have denied. What do you think it is?"

Sam leaned over to Niles and whispered, "What is that?"

"I don't know, but I will find out," Niles whispered back.

Sam held up his watch and typed a message.

"You can text on this thing?" Niles gazed down at his.

"Yes. You should play with it sometime. It does all sorts of cool stuff." He read the message. "It's a Valderonian battle cruiser. Is that bad?"

"Ask her."

He typed in the next message. "Yes, it's very bad. She says don't contact her anymore. She's hiding from it."

"How about us?"

Sam typed again. "She says sorry. She can't decloak to let you in or they'll see her."

"Can they see me?"

He typed again. He waited until class ended. "Gina isn't responding."

"Great. Well, I know where I'm going to spend the next twenty years of my life." Niles sighed heavily. "Oh, twenty-two years. It's going to take two years to get back to Valderon."

"Let's not give up that easy. We'll go talk to your dad. I'm sure he'll have some good ideas."

That night as Niles rode the bus home, he watched Sam pass them on his scooter. If there was a problem on the way home tonight, there would be no saving him this time. He felt abandoned by Gina. He had tried several times to call and text her, but she wasn't answering. He felt like going out into the woods at the back of the house and knocking on her door. That would only bring the Valderonians down on her too. He decided not to. When he arrived home, as soon as he stepped through the door, his mom handed him a shovel.

"Dad says to meet him out back."

Niles headed back to find Sam and his father digging a hole. "What's going on?"

"When are these aliens coming?" George asked.

Niles felt a little hurt. He was half-blood of the men that were coming to get him. He tucked in his feelings. "I don't know. Soon, I suspect."

"We need to dig fast then." The three of them dug an eight-foot-deep hole and then his father put thin branches and pine boughs over it. "I'm figuring that they will come to the place where the tracker was last. Sam told me all about it. Then they will march this way because this is the only house around. That's when you will stand and entice them forward. They will fall into the pit where we'll be able to negotiate with them." They sat down at the edge of the hole. George had his shotgun sitting against a tree near them. He had never seen one before, but he figured it was some kind of weapon.

"Sounds good to me," Niles swallowed involuntarily.

"Wait, can they just beam you up?"

Niles' forehead creased. "Beam me up?"

"Yeah, like in the movies. They lock onto you and transport you up to their ship."

Niles shook his head. "They don't have that technology nor do I believe it exists. No, they will come down in a shuttle and bring me to their ship."

"Good. Then my plan might work."

They sat there for two hours just on the other side of the hole. George finally spoke up. "I always wanted a son. I was okay having two daughters but I thought that having a son to do projects with would be fun. I didn't know when I finally got one I'd be fixing spacecraft and waiting to fight off aliens." It caused both Sam and Niles to laugh. George's phone went off a few minutes later. When he stuck it back in his pocket, he said, "That was your mom. She says something was coming out from space so they scrambled two F-15s from Mountain Home Air Force Base, but by the time they made it here, the thing they were tracking disappeared."

"They've landed then and cloaked their shuttle," Niles said. He stood up.

"It's showtime," Sam said. He stood up next to Niles and George.

Chapter Twenty
Alien Invasion

Dark shapes walked cautiously through the trees. Niles shouted out in Valderonian, *"Here I am, come and get me."*

They pointed their weapons at him. "*Don't try anything foolish.*" They didn't rush forward.

"What did they say?" George asked.

Niles didn't answer George but continued talking to the intruders. "*You had your chance. I'm leaving now. I didn't want to get arrested for something I didn't do anyway.*" He turned and took several steps. The five Valderonians ran forward and all fell into the pit.

George picked up the shotgun and pointed it at them. "Drop your weapons or get blasted."

Niles came back to the hole. "*He says to drop your weapons and raise your hands. You are trapped and he's the only way you have of getting out of that hole.*"

They did as he said.

After dropping in the ladder, George motioned for them to sit around the fire pit, shotgun always at the ready. Sam started the fire and they all leaned back in their seats. "*You will not be burned. Sam just wants to stay warm.*"

They relaxed. "What do you keep saying?" George asked.

"They thought we were going to burn them."

"Oh." George turned to them. "We will not hurt you unless you try to take my son."

"*He says he will not hurt you unless you try to take his son.*"

The leader of the group frowned. "*You are not his son. The criminal Craig is your father.*"

"*He is the husband of my mother. This man has been more of a father to me in the short time I've known him than the criminal Craig has been over the many years I lived with him*".

The man nodded.

"What's he saying?" George asked.

"He doesn't think you're my father but I set him straight."

"Good. What can we do to get them to go away and never come back?"

"He wants you to leave."

"I cannot leave unless I bring you with me. You are a criminal too."

Niles shook his head. *"I know I was found guilty but I wasn't given a chance to defend myself. If you track the money you will see not a single galactic credit has been touched by me. I didn't know the accounts existed. I'm not guilty."*

The man held out his hands and stood up slowly. *"I will verify your story and if it's true, then I will tear up your arrest warrant. For now, I must go back to my shuttle and then back to the ship."*

"It's okay, Dad, they are leaving for now," Niles added. *"Don't fly between the moon and the Earth. The humans can see you if you do. They sent out fighter jets to try and stop your shuttle."*

The man gasped. *"We didn't know they had that capability. We will be more careful. Where is your father anyway?"*

"I don't know. He sent out a message demanding his ship back. I can't show you as my ship is hiding from you and won't uncloak."

He laughed. *"Tell Gina our sensors can detect cloaked ships and we have seen her the whole time. That is how we knew where to come."*

Niles punched his watch. "Did you hear that, Gina?"

"Fine, the transmission came from Trajous three. He was orbiting the planet at the time. I don't think he stayed there."

"She says…"

"I know what she said."

Niles took a step back. "You can speak English?"

The man shrugged. "Yes."

"Then why didn't you from the start?"

"I wanted my men to know what was going on. They don't speak English." He bowed and the group left.

Sam's eyes were wide. "Wow, I saw real aliens." George cleared his throat and nodded at Niles. "Oh, I mean besides Niles," Sam added. "He's only half-alien so that hardly counts."

"What happens now?" George asked.

"They are looking into seeing if the sentence they passed down on me was justified. I guess only time will tell. I'm going to talk to Gina. She abandoned me in my hour of need."

"I'll come, too," Sam said.

As they neared, they watched the Valderonian shuttle take off. It had been next to Gina. They stepped towards her, and she decloaked. "Sorry," she said.

"I need to make sure you won't abandon me again." Niles didn't enter but stood there with his arms folded glaring at her.

"I can show you the flight of the shuttle as it nears the battle cruiser," Gina replied.

"That sounds cool," Sam said. He ducked into the spaceship.

Niles rolled his eyes but then followed Sam into the ship. They watched as the shuttle docked with the battle cruiser in deep space. Then the battle cruiser went deeper into the solar system.

"Well, that was exciting," Niles said.

"Maybe not for you, but I'm a kid from North Idaho and I've never seen anything like that before."

"You'll get to see it again when they come back."

Sam gasped. "They're coming back?"

Chapter Twenty-One
An Angry Father

It was a funny feeling going back to school after the encounter with the Valderonians. Niles didn't know what his appeal would be, but the leader of the group seemed to think Niles was right. It could all land on deaf ears and another group of them could come down and take him away at any moment. Even out of class.

He knew they wouldn't fall for the same trap twice. Gina hadn't been any help last time. He waited until he was between classes to call her. "Any movement from the battlecruiser?"

"No, they seem to be happily orbiting the planet at a distance."

"Thanks." He turned to find Darcy standing behind him.

"Who are you talking to? She has a nice voice."

What was that voice inflection, Niles wondered. Jealousy?

"I was talking to my computer. Her voice is synthesized. The same computer I was talking to when you eavesdropped on me in the library."

"Oh." She smiled. "There is a Sadie Hawkins dance in two weeks. I would like you to come with me."

"Sadie Hawkins? Who is that?"

She put her hands on her hips. "She's a cartoon character, but that doesn't matter. Are you going to come to the dance with me or not?"

"I don't know how to dance."

"Oh, well if that's your only excuse, I can teach you how to dance. Great, I'll see you then." She hugged him and then walked on down the hall.

Let's see, I could be in stasis on my way back to Valderon to face trial over my father's criminal activities. Would that count as an excuse? He watched her leave.

Sam came up to him. "What was that all about?"

"Darcy just invited me to some dance called Sadie Hawkins."

"Oh, Alyce invited me to that dance too."

"Wait, you're going with my twin sister?"

Sam's eyes narrowed. "Half-sister. I said yes, so I am going. Is there a problem? You didn't even know she existed two months ago now suddenly you're the protective brother? Then you get asked by the girl of my dreams and don't want to go? Did you say yes at least?"

Niles held up his hands. "I didn't say yes or no, she just assumed a yes."

"That sounds like Darcy. Hmm, I have an idea."

They met over at Niles' house after school. They waited until Alyce walked down the hall to talk. "I think we should take them out to dinner before the dance," Sam said.

"That's your idea?"

Lucia entered the room. "I didn't mean to eavesdrop, but no, you can't do that. The girls asked you out. They are in charge. You go along with what they want to do." Shaking her head, she left the room.

"Okay, so it wasn't such a good idea after all." Sam leaned back in his chair. "I have to get home anyway. Say, I've eaten over here a couple of times. Do you want to come to my house for dinner? I'll have to check with my mom, first. She always cooks too much anyway."

Niles shrugged. "Sure."

While Sam asked his mother, Niles told Janice of the plan. "It's okay by me. Alyce has invited Darcy over anyway to plan the Sadie Hawkins dance. I'm sure she'll be glad you're not around."

"That almost makes me want to stay."

Janice pointed at the door. "Go on, you two."

Niles hopped in the back of the scooter for a ride into town. He knew the route well, it had been the same one he had followed that day, and made sure Sam wasn't hit by the box truck. They arrived at a nice single-story home in a neighborhood.

"Mom, Dad, this is Niles."

Sam's dad scowled. "I've met him. I don't want him in my house. Get out."

Niles turned and stepped toward the door. "Stop," Sam's mom said. She put her hands on her hips as she faced the father. "I told him he could eat with us. He's Sam's friend now. We are all going to eat and be nice about it."

"Come on, Dad," Sam said. "He's a good guy."

"Supper is ready, let's all come and eat and be nice."

His father stood up but glared at Niles on the way by when no one else was watching. They sat down to a dinner of chicken, rice, and seasoned tomato sauce all in the same dish.

The mother dished out some food to everyone. The father didn't say a word all through dinner. Sam's mother asked. "So, where did you live before you came here, Niles?"

"Mom, Niles doesn't want to talk about it."

"It's okay. I'm from a town far, far away called Graghtin."

"What country is that?" she asked.

"It's in Valderon."

"That place doesn't exist," Sam's dad interjected.

"I assure you it does. I grew up there."

Sam's mother glared at his father. "Honey, you aren't very good at geography. Let's just eat."

After dinner, Sam's dad excused himself. Sam and Niles helped clean up. When Niles stepped outside, Sam's dad blocked his way. "You hurt my son. Now you're going to pay." He took a swing at Niles, but he easily sidestepped it.

"I don't want to hurt you."

"Dad, stop," Sam stepped outside and tried to get between them, but the dad pushed him to the ground and took another swing at Niles. Niles hit him in the gut, sending him to the ground doubled up.

"I didn't want to hurt him."

Sam checked on his father. "Why did you have to go and do something stupid like that?"

His dad moaned. Niles came over. "Are you all right?"

"Oof." He caught his breath. "I will be."

"Let's go," Sam pulled Niles toward the scooter. "Dad's all about family honor. I keep telling him his family honor will get him killed someday."

"I didn't want to hurt him."

"He was being stupid. He won't be doing that again."

Chapter Twenty-Two
Dinner for Four

Janice greeted Niles when he arrived home. "How was dinner?"

"Good." He tried to go to his room, but she put her hand on his arm. "What's wrong?"

"Sam's dad tried to hit me. I had to defend myself. I'm upset about how many fights I get into down here. That never happened on Valderon. I'm afraid I hurt him badly."

"I'll call over there and see." She went out the front door to call.

Nilcs lay down on his bed. He thought about his life and how everything was different. On Valderon, he had never gotten into a fight and now he had been in two. *Of course I wasn't in a fight. I lived with servants and private tutors.* He shook his head. He didn't have classmates like he did now.

After knocking, his mother came into Niles' room. "He's okay, all but his ego.

After you left Sam's mom started yelling at his dad and it didn't let up until I called. It may have started again after I hung up. I don't know. Wait I'm getting a call. Hello?"

She handed Niles the phone. "It's for you."

"Hello?" Niles said.

"I'm sorry. I shouldn't have harassed you when you first arrived and I shouldn't have picked a fight with you. I *really* shouldn't have picked a fight with you."

"Are you okay?"

"I'm going to have a giant bruise tomorrow, I'm sure. Thanks for asking."

Niles stared at the phone before he handed it back. "That was Sam's dad. He said sorry."

"Oh, good. I'm glad that's over. I see I forgot to get you a phone. I'll take you right after school tomorrow. A boy your age needs his own phone."

"Thanks."

During school the next day the math teacher wrote a long equation on the board. "I know this is over the head of most of you. I want you to figure out the process of solving it. Sam, what is the first step I should take?"

Niles tried to mouth the answer to Sam, but he wasn't getting it. He finally shrugged. "I don't know."

"Why don't we have Niles tell you then, as he tried to do while you were struggling?" Niles sighed and then told him how to begin to solve it. After class, the teacher motioned for Niles to stay. "How did you get so much smarter than all my other students?"

"I had a very advanced education with tutors all my life."

"So, why aren't you still seeing these tutors of yours?"

"My father sent me away when he had legal troubles. I'm living with my mom now."

"It must be hard to be going to public school when you had private tutors all your life."

"No. It turns out I was lonely. I just didn't realize it."

"Well, it's good to have you in class. I need a teacher's assistant. You are too advanced to be taking this class anyway. Are you willing to do that?"

"Yes." Niles nodded.

"Good. We can play with advanced math theories while the rest of the class struggles with the basics."

"Sounds good."

The teacher cleared his throat. "Are you going to the Sadie Hawkins dance on Friday?"

"Yes."

"I'll see you then. I get the pleasure of chaperoning it." The teacher gave him a brief smile and then went back into his office.

When Friday rolled around, Darcy pulled up in the driveway. She had picked up Sam on the way over. Alyce and Niles walked out and sat in the car. She drove them to Paul Bunyan Burger. "This is all the fancy dinner Alyce and I could afford," she admitted.

"I love this place," Sam said.

As they entered, Niles looked at the menu. "What's a burger?"

Darcy gasped, but then covered her mouth. "That's right, you're not from around here. It's called a hamburger."

"I've had ham before."

"This isn't that," Sam said. "It's made out of beef."

"Oh, beef comes from cows. Bacon, I've had before. It comes from pigs. I guess I'll try a double bacon burger with cheese then."

"I'll have the same," Sam said.

"Do you want fries with that?" Darcy could tell by the look on his face he didn't know what that was either. "Never mind, I'll go ahead and order those. If you don't like them I'm sure the rest of us will have no problem polishing them off. I'm going to get you a vanilla milkshake, too. Look, you get to experience three new things today."

"Sounds good."

The girls ordered four double bacon cheeseburgers with fries and shakes. When they sat down with their food, Darcy said, "Don't drink your shakes yet. I'm going to let Niles taste them all before. I grabbed some plastic spoons from the counter. Here, Niles, mine is strawberry. What do you think?"

"Oh, it's cold. I wasn't expecting that. It's good."

"Mine's banana." Alyce slid her shake over.

Niles shook his head. "I don't like that one."

"Weird," Darcy creased her forehead. "You would think that twins would have similar tastes."

Sam handed him a spoonful of his. "Try this. It's cherry. You can't go wrong with cherry."

"That's good." He tasted his own shake. "This is good too. I think I like this one the best." He tried his fries and then his burger. "This is so good. Thanks for bringing me here."

After they ate, Darcy announced. "It's time to go to the dance."

Chapter Twenty-Three
The Dance

Loud country music greeted them as they entered the gym of the high school. Red and orange streamers hung from the roof down to the basketball hoops. There were straw bales around the walls to sit on. A table full of pies sat at one end of the room. On the other side stood a photo booth decorated like a barn.

Darcy grabbed Niles' hand and led him out to the dance floor. "Here is what you do. Let your body move how it wants to. Nobody cares." She started moving her hips and feet. "Until the line dances play. They're a little more complicated."

He mimicked her as best as he could. Soon Alyce and Sam were dancing right next to them. Alyce smiled and nodded so he kept doing what he was doing. That song ended and Niles saw other couples walk toward the side, but when he tried to follow, Darcy grabbed his arm. "There will be another song soon." They stayed for the next three songs, but then a line dance came on so she led him towards the pies.

The four of them sat on straw bales and ate their slices of pie. After taking a bite, Niles pointed at the pie with his fork. "I like this, too."

"Boy, you've had a lot of new culinary experiences today." Darcy waited until he finished to drag him out on the floor for a slow song. "You put your hand on my hip and your other on my shoulder." She smiled at him.

"All the things I've missed since my father kidnapped me."

She stopped mid dance. "You were kidnapped?"

"Yes. I thought you knew."

She shook her head. "I didn't, wow. Where did he take you?"

"Across the galaxy. It took two years to travel there."

"Wow, that's crazy." She started dancing again. "You poor thing."

"It wasn't so bad. I had private tutors, cooks, servants, and a valet. I wasn't suffering."

"That's good." The song ended so they headed toward the side and sat down next to Sam and Alyce.

"What do you think?" Sam asked.

"I'm having a blast."

Alyce sighed. "Another line dance song. I don't know how to dance to those."

"Let's try," Niles stood up and pulled up Darcy and Alyce too. Sam followed them. They stayed on the sidelines mimicking the dancers and occasionally laughing as they ran into each other. The song ended before they had perfected it. "I guess we'll have to wait until the next line dance song."

Darcy shook her head. "They are all different. The next one isn't going to be like the one we just tried to do."

"Oh. that does complicate things."

"I'm going in for round two of the pies." Sam and the girls walked away.

"How are you doing, young Niles?" He turned to see his math teacher standing behind him.

"I'm having fun. I only wish I knew all the line dances."

"Think of it as a math problem. You do the steps, then turn and do the same steps again. It's repetition after the first turn."

He watched for a minute. "Oh, is that all there is to it?"

"Yes."

He started dancing alone on the side of the gym. When the group came back, he had the latest line dance down.

"Very good," Alyce said. "I can never get those." She handed him a piece of pie. "Try this one. It's cherry."

"Oh, that's very good. Thank you."

"What type of fruits do you have on your planet?" Darcy asked.

"Shh," Alyce said and then had the group move away from everyone else.

"Oops, sorry."

"We have mostly green ones. The red ones are considered poisonous so we don't eat them. They grow wild, like weeds between some of the cities. The other fruits are farmed."

"Oh, what do they taste like?"

"Sweet but bland in comparison to yours."

Both Sam's and Niles' watches lit up. Niles answered his. "The battle cruiser is moving closer and two shuttles have left the cargo bay. They are headed towards us, Gina said."

"We have to go," Sam moved towards the door.

Chapter Twenty-Four
More Aliens

Darcy drove towards Sam's house, "No, we have to go to Niles' place and check out the backyard. Hurry."

"Okay," she said. "What's going on?"

"We have to stop the aliens."

Her eyes went round. "More aliens." She hit the gas.

All seemed quiet when they arrived. They headed straight to the woods behind the house. Sam tried to contact Gina, but then shook his head when he didn't get a response. They crept towards where she was.

"When did we get a hen house?" Alyce said.

Fifteen soldiers rushed forward and surrounded the group pointing their weapons at them. They raised their hands instinctively.

"It's a cloaked ship," Niles whispered back.

"Quiet," one of the soldiers said, then pointed toward the fire pit and said something in Valderonian.

The soldiers marched the four of them toward the fire. Lucia, Janice, and George were sitting around it along with ten soldiers. "Sorry, son. They got the drop on us."

The soldiers pointed for the four of them to sit down. The commander stood next to the fire. "I love open flame. I'm going to reintroduce it on my planet when I get home."

"What do you want of us?" George asked.

"Oh, I don't want you. I just want Yan Dak."

"Who?" George asked.

"That's my Valeronian name," Niles admitted. "I thought you were going to state my case. I've never touched the money."

"I did state your case, that is why you're getting a new trial back on Valderon."

"But it will take two years to get there and two years to get back," Niles protested.

"Can't you do it remotely?" George asked.

"What do you mean?"

"Could they hold the trial over the transmitters so he doesn't have to lose four years out of his life only to be acquitted?"

The leader scratched his chin. "That's a good idea. I'll talk to Valderon. I didn't relish the idea of flying that far only to come back. Still, it would have been nice to see my home planet again."

He left, but his men stayed.

"I have to get home," Darcy said after an hour.

Niles relayed the message to the Valderonians, but they shook their heads. "You aren't going anywhere."

"I need to call my mom then." She pulled out her phone but one of the soldiers grabbed it.

"I don't think they want you to do that either." Niles spoke to them in their own language, *"She needs to call her mother so she won't worry."*

"She needs to wait until our leader comes back," The soldier said simply.

"He said wait." Niles stood up and stretched.

When he sat back down, Darcy slid down the bench and snuggled up to him. "Hold me, I'm scared." Niles put his arm around her.

The leader came back a few minutes later. "They have agreed to try you over the transmitters. They have assigned you a lawyer. He will meet you tomorrow morning."

"Thank you," George said. "Can these kids go home? It's getting late."

He shook his head. "They will have to stay overnight. In the morning, Niles will meet with his lawyer and then the trial will commence. It shouldn't take too long."

"Will he be properly represented?" George asked.

"His lawyer is a friend of mine. He's the best."

"Thank you."

That night Sam and Darcy were able to phone home and ask to spend the night. Darcy slept in Alyce's room and Sam slept on the couch. Niles lay in bed staring at the ceiling all night. His future hung in the balance and even if they wanted to put him in prison for a month, it would be a four-year trip there and back again.

He had settled in to his new home easily. He would miss the people who showed him love. George watched out for him and knew the right questions to ask. When a knock came on his door, he checked the time. It was time for breakfast and he hadn't slept a wink.

Chapter Twenty-Five
Shot and shot again.

When Niles came out of his room, his family sat around the table having breakfast. Around them stood five soldiers. His Mom motioned him over. "I hope your friends don't want anything to eat. I don't have enough food for everyone."

"I'm sure they have their own."

The leader came in a minute later. "Your lawyer wants to meet with you. His name is Yaren."

"Okay. Where?"

"We'll use Gina's transmitter. That way the government can't monitor it."

Niles stood up and both of them headed for Gina. She decloaked as they approached. As they went in, she said, "Someone by the name of Yaren is trying to get a hold of you."
"Put him on."

The monitor beeped to life and a clean-shaven man with brown hair came on. "Ah, there you are. I have been going over the state's case and it's thin. Very thin. I think we can knock that down to five years easily."

Nile folded his arms. "I didn't do anything wrong."

Yaren raised his eyebrows. "It says you opened three accounts in your name and put the Chancellor's money in them."

"I didn't. My father did all that."

"I see. I'll track all that. Thank you for letting me know."

"Thank you for representing me."

"My pleasure. Bye for now." The monitor went off.

As the leader and Niles walked back to the house, Niles thanked him for arranging that one as well.

"When will the trial begin?"

"Soon, very soon."

"Can my friends go home yet?" Niles asked.

"Not yet. I don't want them telling the local authorities that we are here."

"They won't."

"You've tricked us before." The leader walked away.

An hour later, Darcy's father showed up at the house. George let him in. "Why are you keeping our daughter?" he demanded.

"Don't have a choice," George replied. Five of the guards came around the corner and pointed their weapons at him.

"Don't point those things at me." He slapped one of the guns out of the guard's hand. The guard behind Darcy's father shot him. A green blast came out and he screamed as he fell to the ground.

Darcy rushed into the room. "Dad." She leaned down to check on him.

"Wow, that was intense," he said as Darcy helped him up.

"Are you okay?" she asked.

"I will be. Who are these people?"

"They're aliens."

"What?"

"It's okay, Dad. Come sit down." She led him to a chair.

The leader came into the room having been told of the problem by one of the guards. "Who are you?" he asked.

"Who *are* you?"

"You don't need to know who I am."

"Then you don't need to know who I am either.":

"This is my dad. My mom is going to be worried about him. I need to call and tell her he's fine."

"Go ahead, but I need to listen to every word."

She dialed. "Mom, Dad is here. We have to stay and help the Morgan's. We won't be home for a while."

Her dad stood up and yelled into the phone, "Call the police, we're being invaded by aliens."

Another shot rang out and he hit the floor again.

"Don't listen to him, Mom. He has been acting crazy since he arrived. I'll make sure he's okay before I send him home." Darcy paused while her mother talked. "Okay, you know how he gets when his blood sugar gets low. I'll get him something to eat. Love you, Mom."

She helped him up again. "Why did you do that? You know mother would sooner lose a toe than to call the police."

Niles came into the house. He talked to the nearest guard. *"What's going on?"*

"This idiot keeps making us shoot him."

"Who is he?"

The guard shrugged. "Niles," Darcy smiled. Come meet my father."

He was still rubbing the spot where they shot him the second time. "So, you're Niles. I've heard so much about you, over and over again and then some."

Darcy blushed. "Dad."

"It's nice to meet you," Niles replied.

"How is it that you can speak the language of the aliens?"

"This is the language of my countryman."

"Oh, so they are illegal aliens."

"They'll be gone soon. I hope."

"I do too. Those tasers of theirs hurt."

"I wouldn't know. They have never shot me."

"So, are you an illegal alien too?"

"I don't know what that is," Niles replied.

"You were born here, so that makes you a citizen," George answered.

"Oh. How is it that he has countrymen?"

"Dad, stop talking. He was kidnapped. I'll try and explain all this later." Darcy patted his arm.

He turned to the leader. "How long are you going to keep me and my daughter hostage?"

"Until after the trial."

"Who's on trial?"

Niles cleared his throat. "I am."

Chapter Twenty-Six
The Trial

Niles sat down in one of the shuttles. Two guards with weapons poised stood behind him. A large monitor blinked to life. Niles watched as the chancellor in his red robe and shiny crown sat down. His defense attorney sat down to the right of the chancellor and another man in a traditional suit sat down on his left.

They sat in the grand hall, lined with long colorful tapestries and large windows to let in the light.

The chancellor cleared his throat. *"Yan Dak, you are accused of aiding and abetting your father in the embezzlement of funds. You have been sentenced to twenty years in prison. This court is merciful, however. The new plea deal is for ten years served and ten years probation."*

The man to the right of the chancellor spoke next. *"I think, Your Majesty, we can plea it down to ten years."*

"Ten years," the chancellor said. *"Do you accept this deal?"* He turned to

look at Yaren. *"Advise your client to accept this generous offer."*

"We do not accept, Your Majesty. Niles is innocent of all crimes he stands accused of."

The chancellor's jaw dropped. *"Not guilty?"* He turned to the prosecutor at his right. *"How can that be?"*

"He's clearly guilty, Your Majesty. His hand prints are on all the bank documents."

Yaren smiled. *"If I may, your majesty. Here are the cameras from all the banks at the time of the accounts being established. Craig is there alone, all three times."*

"That doesn't prove that he knew about the accounts. He gave Craig his hand stamp," the prosecutor said.

Shaking his head, Yaren replied. *"It doesn't prove that he did know about it either. A hand print could have been obtained while he was sleeping."*

The prosecutor replied. *"In light of the new evidence, we can plea down to five years probation."*

"What does the accused say to five years probation?" the chancellor asked.

Everyone looked at Niles. He had held his tongue up to this point. *"No. I didn't do anything wrong. I want my name cleared."*

"It's a very generous offer," the chancellor insisted. *"How are you going to prove that you had nothing to do with the accounts?"*

The prosecutor shook his head. *"If you don't take the offer, the deal goes away."*

"You know you can't prove he did it," Yaren interrupted. *"Why are you going after him for this?"*

"The chancellor's money was stolen," he replied. *"Someone has to pay."*

"Very well. I have another witness." Yaren pointed to the screen. An image of his father flashed on it.

Oh no! They caught Dad.

Craig spoke, *"My son had nothing to do with the accounts. I took his handprint from him while he slept."*

The prosecutor shook his head and walked out of the hall.

The chancellor nodded. *"Very well. Charges are dismissed."*

The leader led Niles out of the shuttle. "You were right to fight for your innocents."

"Thank you. I guess you'll be headed back to Valderon."

"No, we patrol this section of space. If you need us, tell Gina to call."

"I will do." Niles didn't realize that they were there to stay. "Can I talk to my father?"

"I'll patch you through."

His father's face came over the view screen. "Are you going to be okay Dad?"

Craig frowned. "No, they gave me twenty years hard labor."

"Oh no."

"Don't worry. My investments were making the chancellor money even with the amount I stole. The guy who took my place lost the chancellor's money, so my hard labor is investing the chancellor's money again. This time, they are watching me like a hawk."

"Oh, good. Bye Dad. I'm glad they didn't execute you."

"Me too, bye."

Niles turned to the leader of the troops. "When do you go home?"

"We are here on a five-year mission. It's only been two so we have three more to go. We have to stay on station until another battle cruiser comes to relieve us."

Niles walked into the house and found everyone sitting around. He smiled and said, "They found me not guilty."

A cheer went up.

"Does this mean I can take my daughter and go home?" Darcy's dad asked.

Niles scanned the room but there were no guards left. "I guess it does."

"Great." He stood up.

"'Bye Niles," Darcy said in a super sweet voice and then she winked at him.

Niles blushed. "'Bye."

Lucia teased after they left. "Looks like you have a girlfriend, Niles."

"What can I do about that?" he asked.

"Ah, go with it. Young love is so cute."

When the others went about their Saturday, Sam took Niles aside. "I would like to take another swing around the moon. When can we do that?"

"How about right now?"

They walked back to the yard and Niles checked on the shuttles. "They're gone," he said with a smile.

Gina decloaked and they both came aboard. "We are going around the moon," Sam declared.

"I know," Gina replied. "I can hear you through your watches."

"Remind me to take it off while I go to the bathroom," Sam replied.

"That would be nice."

Niles ignored them and checked the preflight data. "No light or air leaks. Everything is good. Starting engines."

"Roger," Sam replied. Soon they lifted out from between the trees. Hours later they approached the moon.

"I'm going on the back side of it this time so I don't get spotted by that telescope in Hawaii."

Both Sam and Niles agreed. When they reached the backside, Sam pointed. "What is that?"

"Scanning," Gina said. "Object identified. It's a large probe."

"Why would the Valderonians send out another probe?" Niles asked.

"They didn't. It's someone else's."

"Is this going to be a problem?" Sam asked.

"Yes," she said.

Guardian of Earth
Adventures of Niles Morgan

Book Two

Chapter One
Alien Probe

Niles Morgan heart raced as he sat in his bed staring at the ceiling. He didn't know what to do. Sam and Niles had seen a probe circling the moon from a hostile, space-based, race. His sidekick Sam wanted to ram it like they had the Valderon probe, but Gina, their spaceship, had told them they were risking a serious hull breach if they did. This probe was five times larger.

Sam and Niles had flown around the probe so Gina could figure out whose it was. She named a race that Niles had never heard of. She seemed upset but didn't say anything. She made them fly quickly back to Earth and as soon as Sam and he walked out, she cloaked back into her old shed disguise.

By the time the two of them walked back into the house, the sun had set. Niles' mom, Janet, drove Sam home.

Niles couldn't take it anymore. He typed into his watch, "Where is that probe from?"

Gina didn't answer him. He tried again. Still no answer. Getting upset, he headed into the forest at the back of the house. He went up to the shed and kicked it. "Ow," Gina said through his watch.

"Whose probe is that?"

"Quiet, they'll hear me."

He kicked her again. "Decloak."

She did a minute later. "What do you want?"

"I want answers. Is the earth in danger? Whose probe is that and should I be worried?"

"The probe is from Karatar. They are not friendly to the Valderons. I don't think they have had any dealings with Earth."

"Yet. They are spying on us and you're afraid of them. I want to talk to that Valderon battle cruiser if it isn't too far away by now."

"Step in." She cloaked back into a shed as soon as he did. The screen came on and a man's face filled it.

"Hello, Yan, I mean, Niles. This is Commander Tarris."

"Sorry, I guess I never asked your name after all of our interactions."

"I don't blame you. I kept trying to arrest you. What do you need?"

"There's a Karatar probe on the back side of the moon and it's spying on earth."

Tarris stared at the monitor for a minute. "That isn't a good thing. They are the ones that caused our planet to be so arid. Before we were a space-bound race, they sent their cloud gatherers to suck our clouds out of our skies. It caused an overall fifteen-degree higher, on average, temperature increase, and areas of rich farmland dried up. Millions of our inhabitants died. This is why we don't have beautiful lakes like the one that I saw from the window in your mother's house. We will head back to your planet right away."

"Thank you."

"Tell Gina to uncloak. She can't hide from this problem. We'll need help."

Niles thought he heard a nervous cringe sounds from Gina. "Just tell us when we need to go."

"I will." Tarris turned to one of his monitors and clicked a few buttons. "We'll be there in two days. I don't see anything on our long-range sensors. So far they have only sent a probe. See you in a couple of days."

"Thanks."

The screen went blank. Gina said, "No, we can't fight the Karatars. We should flee. There's another inhabitable planet only a year away. Let's go."

"We're not fighting anyone. We just trying to prevent them from destroying this planet. Besides, I have no galactic credits anymore since they caught my father. I have nowhere to go."

"Fine, I'm calling Sam then."

"No, don't. He can't miss any school. I can handle this on my own."

She sighed. As he headed back to the house, the dogs came out and milled around him. He petted each one in turn. They followed him into the house.

Even with the brave face he wore in front of Gina, his heart raced. *How do I get myself into these situations?*

Janet stood over the stove cooking breakfast when he walked in. "Where have you been?" She asked.

"Out back. I'm trying to solve a problem."

"This doesn't have to do with the probe on the far side of the moon that Sam told me about on the way home yesterday, does it?"

"It has everything to do with it."

Made in United States
Troutdale, OR
02/17/2025

28983188R00096